Back to the BURGH
and BEYOND

The 's Nest Mysteries

Book One:

Back to the BURGH and BEYOND

by

C.S. McDONALD

ISBN: 9798684160080

Contents

Chapter One

Back to the Burgh

T*hump, thump-thump.* Potholes. Alexa Owl's hometown of Pittsburgh, Pennsylvania, was famous for many things: the Steelers, the Pirates, the Penguins, steel mills, Heinz ketchup, pierogies, the Klondike bar, and potholes. Obviously, there was a doozie of a pothole on the street directly outside of her new place of business, The Owl's Nest Couturier Shoppe. Of course, she hadn't hit the pothole on purpose. She hadn't noticed the *chasm* because she was too busy trying to parallel park her Lexus SUV while some jerk in a red Jaguar was blaring his horn at her. When he managed to zip past, he yelled something out the window she didn't care to decipher.

Well, welcome back to the Burgh.

Alexa had left Pittsburgh seventeen years ago. Although, she hadn't gone terribly far, just to Columbus, Ohio, and of course, she came home to visit her parents... semi-often. After graduating high school, she set off for Ohio State University to study fashion design and earn a degree in business management as well. She married Dennis Owl, a real estate broker, when she was twenty-five, and divorced him almost a year ago. After the divorce was official, she decided she needed a change in scenery. Hence, her return to the Steel City, the Burgh, and her new business venture, The Owl's Nest.

Her now ex-husband Dennis was a wealthy man, and her divorce settlement was most generous and satisfying. Dennis kept the brokerage firm and their five-bedroom, four-bath, six-car-garage palace. In return, he purchased an abandoned building that once housed a pub on Penn Avenue at the very edge of the Strip District downtown. The Strip is made up of a half-mile-square area filled with businesses, boutiques, food markets, restaurants, and nightlife. It is definitely one of the most visited areas of Pittsburgh, making it a perfect location for Alexa's shop.

Dennis had paid to completely refurbish the defunct Lazy Hound Pub to suit her tailor shop's needs, including a private fitting room for clients, a huge sewing room, and a charming suite for bridal fittings and alterations. He'd hired a separate contractor and an interior designer who worked together exclusively on the apartment up-stairs for Alexa to reside. After all the time spent within the confines of a mansion in the middle of suburbia, she was ready to live in among the ebb and flow of a city. Along with the new shop and apartment, she had been awarded a hefty cash defrayal. Not to mention, she was rid of Dennis and all things very Dennis. Unfortunate-ly, including friends. It seemed all of their "close" friends had been part of *his* settlement.

"I'm so sorry to hear that you and Dennis are getting

a divorce." "If there's anything I can do, don't hesitate to call." "We really must keep in touch." "Let's have lunch sometime." These were the hollow sentiments she heard over and over again. And of course, her text messages weren't answered, nor voice mail messages returned.

Alexa had been too busy with the business of selling and closing her tailor shop in Columbus to travel to Pittsburgh to oversee any of the work being done on the building. Her shop had been very successful, and many of her clientele planned to make the three-hour trek up route 70 for special-occasion garments. Alexa followed the progress, and sometimes regression, of the project via photographs, emails, text messages, and a few video conferences with the designer, Lydia. She would make decisions for Lydia or the contractor to carry out. Dennis would pay for said decisions. She liked the arrangement—*very* much. Today would be the first time she'd actually lay eyes on her new shop and apartment. Lydia had called two days ago to say all of the furniture, personal effects, and items from her old shop that she did not leave behind for the new owner had arrived. Perfect.

The red Jaguar was now stuck behind a delivery truck about a half block away. She could hear the long-suffering blast of the vehicle's horn. Someone was either in a very big hurry, or they were simply an ignoramus in a fancy car. Alexa favored the latter.

It had been a long drive from Columbus. She left the burden of makeup for another day and tossed her cinnamon brunette hair atop her head in a messy bun. She'd decided long ago that yoga pants, an oversized Ohio State T-shirt, and a pair of flip-flops were the best, or at least the most comfortable, traveling attire. She'd made a quick stop at a travel-station just outside Zanesville to purchase a cup of coffee. Coffee, another must-have for long drives, morning commutes, or a trip to the mall—actually, coffee was simply a must-have. Period.

Taking the last sip of coffee from her travel mug, she switched the ignition off, then stuffed the mug back into the cup holder. She grabbed up her purse and the leather laptop case and opened the door to slip from her SUV. The sultry heat of July bounced from the pavement. Wasting no time, she hurried to the sidewalk to gaze upon her new place of business. Her lips curled. Well done. This shop had a different look than the one she'd left behind in Columbus. This shop had a Pittsburgh charm to it.

Like many of the old structures in Pittsburgh, the building was tall and narrow. An awning of rich raspberry tones shaded the large display window and doorway. Bold lettering above the canopy broadcasted "The Owl's Nest Couturier Shoppe." Alexa was pleased with the frosted curly curvy etched design along the margin of the window. Lydia must've decided the window needed something to dress it up until Alexa's arrival. She had placed one of Alexa's many black velvet dress forms on the generous sill and decorated the form with a lovely pink silk corsage. The door's window was etched the same as the display window, announcing "Alexa Owl, Seamstress." She could feel her heartbeat kicking up. It was definitely time to go inside and have a look around.

Alexa shaded her eyes with her hand to peer up at the windows above the shop, the windows of her apartment. She blinked, then stretched her chin forward trying to get a better look. Was that a cat sitting in one of the windows? A white cat? She took a step forward, then sideways in an attempt to get a better angle. No...there was nothing there. What a relief. She was terribly allergic to cats. As a child she'd so wanted a cat. Her heart said yes. Her sinuses said *no*!

She fished through her purse for the key to the shop, then slid it into the lock, pushed the door open, and stepped inside. Pressing a hand to her chest, she let out a sigh of sheer delight. Two majestic crystal chandeliers dangled over the open area where a freestanding full-length triple mirror stood. A cream-colored French provincial sofa with a tufted ottoman flanked by two overstuffed floral chairs sat about ten feet back from the mirror. The old hardwood floor had been sanded and buffed to a brilliant glow.

Alexa set the leather case against the wall and strolled through the area, taking in the grandeur, then made her way across the shop to the original, long cherry bar. At first, she wanted the bar removed, but the contractor and Lydia talked her into keeping it. The computer sat at one end, while they had set up a lovely coffee bar at the other, close to the window. Behind the entire length of the bar were mirrored shelves where the former proprietors had kept bottles of liquor. The shelves would now display jewelry and possibly bridal accessories. She'd make those decisions over the weekend. In the middle of the shelves was an antique dumbwaiter used to send things from the bar to the apartment above, now her apartment. It took little coercing to persuade her to keep the waiter—it could come in handy. The contractor had installed a carved

5

cherry door over the waiter. The rich wood tones glistened in the lights set above the mirrored shelves. Alexa opened the door to find a fresh, clean car and a button off to the left. She pressed the button and the car ascended slowly to stop somewhere in a wall in her apartment. She imagined the kitchen area. She pressed the button again and the car descended. Cool.

To the far right of the bar and at the farthest reach of the room was a door that led to an office and a small kitchen, and just beyond that an open staircase flanked by a chunky cherry railing that led to her apartment. A stand with a sign that read No Entry was stationed at the bottom of the stairs.

Along the farthest wall of the shop stood a line of black velvet dress forms, five in all. The forms stood like elegant ladies of the manor waiting for fabric to be draped over them, fitted, then transformed into fine apparel. Lydia had swathed a yellow tailor's measuring tape around each form's neck like a scarf. Nice touch. Behind the forms was a door that led to a huge sewing room. Alexa decided she'd wait until tomorrow to check that out.

Absolutely giddy with the large space, Alexa could hardly wait to check out the private fitting rooms. She hurried across the shop to the first door. This room would be a general fitting room. She flung the door open and gasped. This room featured a full-length triple mirror with a platform for the client to stand upon while a pair of slacks or a long dress was measured for hemming. A red camelback sofa with rolled armrests was positioned on the far wall. Very elegant. But the room she was most excited to see was the bridal fitting room. She made haste from the general fitting room to a set of double doors. Throwing the doors open, she found a round platform for the bride to stand on while admiring her long wedding gown draped around her in the full-length triple mirror. The room featured a wine bar and a blue damask Chippendale camelback sofa. A gold candlestick chandelier hung overhead from the vaulted ceiling. The floor was covered in a lovely cream carpet.

"Well, it looks like you didn't only dream about success. Looks like you worked for it, and here it is," a woman's voice called out in a heavy Irish accent.

Alexa froze. She did not recognize the voice. She was pretty sure it couldn't be her interior designer. Lydia was from Boston, and her accent was *very* Bostonian. With measured steps she made her way to the door to peek out into the main area of the shop, where she found a short, tubby woman with a snowy mound atop her head, setting a cake on the bar. She reached into a bright red tote bag slung over her right arm and pulled out a bottle. Alexa believed it to be a liquor bottle—Jameson, a fine Irish whiskey.

The woman was on the short side. She wore a pair of black slacks, beige orthopedic shoes, and an oversized, three-quarter-length sleeve, lavender blouse with the collar flipped up. She went about setting up small paper plates, plastic forks, napkins, and two shot glasses on the bar as if she were about to celebrate with an old, familiar friend.

"Hello...can I help you?" Alexa asked. Her tone was hesitant but cordial.

The old woman turned. Her smile stretched all the

way up to brown eyes. She had the classic look of anyone's grandmother. "I stopped in to welcome you and raise a glass or two in celebration of your new business. Come now, I've made one of me best cakes, Irish whiskey chocolate cake. There's no doubt about it, they're two of the finest ingredients God ever gave man, whiskey and chocolate. 'Course, I only use Jameson. It's the best Irish whiskey, ya know."

Alexa was a bit taken aback by the woman's antics, but there was something undeniably adorable about her. Magical. "I'm sorry, do I know you?" she asked as she drew closer.

The woman clapped her hands together. "Where's me manners? I'm Wynona Mulaney, or as me friends call this old Irish girl, *Winnie*." She hitched her chin toward the door. "And you're Alexa Owl. I'm so pleased to make your acquaintance, Alexa." Without hesitation, she retrieved a cake-cutting knife from the tote. The woman came totally prepared. There was certainly something to respect about a woman with a plan. She sliced two generous pieces of cake, placed them on the plates she'd positioned on the bar, then set straight to opening the bottle of Jameson.

The old Irish woman had definitely piqued Alexa's interest. She made her way over to stand next to Winnie while she poured the whiskey into the shot glasses, then handed one to Alexa. "The old place looks grand, and I love how they sanded out all the rough spots in the bar." Winnie lifted her glass in a toast. "May the best day of your past be the worst day of your future." With that, she flicked the whiskey down her throat. An action Alexa felt Winnie was no stranger to.

"Thank you." Alexa drank her whiskey, then, after wincing for several seconds, she managed in a choked voice, "It sounds like you're familiar with this old building."

Winnie handed her a plate. "Ah, it's like an old friend. It is here, in this very building, where I grew up. Me parents, Brian and Molly Mulaney, owned the Lazy Hound Pub from 1943 to 1967. They came to America in 1940 with ten dollars in their pocket, a babe on me mother's hip, and a dream in their hearts. When I was old enough, I washed dishes until it was bedtime. When I was a schoolgirl, I'd come home to the pub, wash a pile of dishes, then I did me homework on a stool, right down there at the end of the bar." She pointed a crooked finger toward the far expanse of the bar. "Then when I was about fourteen, I started serving the tables, and on it went." She dug a plastic fork into her cake and took a bite, closing her eyes, savoring the flavor. "Not bad. Not bad at all, if I do say so me-self. Go on now, have a taste."

Alexa slipped her purse from her shoulder, set it on the bar, then picked up a fork to take a bite of the cake. She'd never tasted anything so delicious or decadent. "This is wonderful, Winnie. I'd love to have the recipe. So...were you the baby on your mother's hip?"

Winnie shot her an affronted look. "'Course not. That would make me...eighty-one. I'll thank ya not to rush it, lass. It's goin' fast enough as it is."

Yep, there was something magical about Wynona Mulaney. Alexa couldn't decide if it was the sparkle in her eyes or the Irish accent tumbling from her lips. She liked Winnie.

9

"The baby was me sister, Elenore, or Ellie, as we used to call her. Then there was Maggie, and I was the youngest."

"Was Maggie's name Margaret?"

"No, just Maggie."

Alexa chuckled to herself. "Do your sisters live locally?"

Winnie smiled. She patted her left chest with her wrinkled, age-spotted right hand. "They live right here, in me heart."

"I'll bet you have all kinds of stories about this place."

"Ah, that I do. Do ya mind if I have a look around, then?"

Alexa lifted a hand. "Be my guest."

Winnie sat her plate on the bar, then slowly made her way across the open area, stopping to gaze at the chandeliers above, and then at her own image in the triple mirror. "Mom saved money so I could go to business school. Learned how to type, take notes, do bookkeeping. I was the only one of me sisters to go to school. Ellie and Maggie got married and had children." She strolled toward the first dressing room and leaned in to have a look. "I worked at the pub and went to the Tepper School of Business. Oh, isn't this nice." She continued along the wall until she came to the bridal fitting room. "Afterward, I worked for the Duquesne Light Company as a bookkeeper until I retired." She peeked into the room. "Good Lord in the morning, isn't this a fancy room."

"You never married?"

Winnie sauntered along the line of dress forms, smoothing her hand over the velvet. "No. Oh, I had me fair share of lovers. But over the years, I found there are three kinds of Irish men who can't begin to understand women: the young, the old, and men of middle age." She raised a justifying hand. "Now, to be fair, that statement doesn't just apply to the Irish."

"It certainly doesn't." Alexa laughed. She took up her purse from the bar. Something inside her told her she'd just found a friend. A good, kind, and most importantly, wise friend. "C'mon, Winnie, I was just about to go upstairs and see my apartment, and I think I'd love for you to come along."

"I thought you'd never ask." She raised a finger in the air. "But first..." She made her way along the bar, grabbed up the bottle of Jameson, the shot glasses, and the cake. She took the items and placed them inside the dumbwaiter. She searched around a bit, then pressed the button. The waiter lifted. Winnie turned. "Why carry them up when we can send them ahead? We used to call the dumbwaiter Charlie. Me mother used to say he was the handiest man in the pub. 'Course, we didn't have a button to send him up, there was a rope. I must say, the button is much better." She closed the door, then patted it. "I'm glad ya kept ol' Charlie around."

Alexa smiled at Winnie's fond memories. "C'mon then, let's go up and see what Lydia's done with my apartment." She ran her hand over the smooth wood finish of the bar as she made her way toward the stairs. She set the No Entry sign aside, then climbed the stairs, admiring the cream carpeting attached to the middle of the cherry stairs. The carpet flowed down the stairs like a graceful waterfall. They came to a four-foot landing where they faced a white, paneled wood door.

"Here we are," Alexa mumbled.

She'd just slid the key into the latch when the there was a loud *crash* from inside the apartment.

Chapter Two

Who's in the Nest?

Alexa pressed through the door, taking several quick steps forward with Winnie on her heels, then she drew up short. She could feel her heart beating like tiny fists inside her chest. Was someone in her apartment or had something simply slipped from a shelf? Warily, she scanned the small foyer. To her right was an arched window that looked out onto 25th Street. Straight ahead was a guest bathroom. To her left, her bedroom, and then a short segue into the main area of the apartment.

Favoring caution, she dug into her purse and pulled out a black Glock 43. Winnie whispered over her shoulder, with trepidation filling her tone, "What's that you've got there?"

Alexa also retrieved her cell phone, then set the purse on the floor near the door. "It's an insurance policy. Don't worry, Winnie, I know how to use it. *If* I need to use it." She handed her the cell phone. "Use this to dial 9-1-1, if things go badly. Now, stay here near the door. I'll check the apartment out." Without further delay, Alexa inched her way toward the bathroom. The door was open. She stepped inside. Off to the right was a large mirror over a double-bowl sink. To the left a lovely stone shower stall and the toilet. She backed out of the bathroom to creep across the foyer and into her bedroom.

If she hadn't been so ill at ease with the current situation, she would have actually enjoyed what she was looking at. Lydia had done an outstanding job with the country French décor she'd requested. French charm oozed from the bedroom. Plump bright floral and plain shams rested against a four-poster queen-sized bed, while smaller throw pillows with floral designs and plain fabric were piled in front. The bedspread was a white embossed floral, and across the foot of the bed lay a red and white buffalo check throw. The darling painting in an antique oval gold frame, *The Story Book*, a portrait of a little girl with a book, by William Bouguereau, hung by a wide, red, crinkled silk ribbon above the nightstand, and below the painting stood a weathered wood-grain lamp. A cream tufted easy chair was positioned beneath long flowing drapes near the window that looked out over the small parking lot behind her shop. She glanced to her extreme right—the walk-in closet, enclosed by hideaway French doors that, at the moment, were closed.

With measured steps, and the pistol at the ready, she crept past the chest of drawers. Alexa grabbed the handle of the closet door to the right and whipped it into its hideaway slot. The door banged the encasement inside the wall, then bounced out a few inches. Finding a light switch she assumed would brighten the closet, Alexa flicked it to the on position. Indeed, the closet lit up. Perfect shelving units and clothing racks lined the walls. She was relieved to find it unoccupied.

She moved along the wall with a bit more confidence toward the bathroom. Stepping inside, she felt the wall for the light, switching it on. Again, she was most pleased with Lydia's work. This bathroom was a larger version of the guest bath. Double-bowl granite sinks with a huge mirror above and a large tub/shower constructed of stone.

Bedroom and baths—all clear. On to the living room and kitchen areas.

"I'll have to assume you didn't find anything. I didn't hear the gun go off or a body hit the floor. And thank the good Lord for both," Winnie commented when Alexa returned to the foyer.

Lowering the gun to her side, Alexa let out a beleaguered sigh. "No. I think something just fell. Let's go look in the living room. I'm pretty sure everything's secure."

"I've got to admit, I took a peek into the bathroom and your bedroom. Your closet is almost bigger than me family's entire apartment."

The two women paused at the archway that led into the living room and kitchen area. Alexa turned. "The contractor said this upper level had three small apartments. He told me the guest bathroom you saw was the only bathroom up here. He assumed it was a communal bath for all three residents."

"And right he would be." Winnie pointed toward the area now designated as Alexa's bedroom suite. "There was a tiny apartment down there. Bobby Starr and his wives occupied that unit."

"His *wives*? Plural? As in, he had more than one?"

Around a chuckle, Winnie replied, "Not all at one time, mind you. But he had more than I can remember. One of his poor wives—" Her voice fell away. Alexa waited for her to finish her sentence, yet by the look on the old Irish woman's face it became apparent she didn't care to continue the thought. Winnie cleared her throat, then gestured to another section of the hall wall. "Right about here there was a door. Mr. and Mrs. Murphy lived in that apartment for many years. They were an old Irish couple. Me parents used to play cards with them every Sunday evening. Business' weren't open on Sundays back in *those* days. They lived there until Mr. Murphy died, then Mrs. Murphy moved in with her daughter."

"Interesting. It's nice to learn the history behind old buildings," Alexa put in as they stepped into the living room. She heard Winnie let out a gasp of pure awe. Alexa knew she was grinning herself. "I don't think I've ever been more pleased with an interior designer."

"This was me family's apartment. And it *never* looked like this."

Alexa had no doubt about Winnie's statement. Straight ahead were two tall windows that looked out over Penn Avenue. Maroon curtains pulled back by tasseled ropes adorned the frames. Between the windows, Lydia had an electric-flame fireplace installed with a whitewashed mantle. A flat-screen TV was stationed above the fireplace.

Beneath a grand crystal chandelier, four white stuffed chairs with fat black and white throw pillows on each were positioned at the four corners of a vintage floral throw rug. A whitewashed table sat in the middle of the cluster. A fresh floral arrangement sat upon the table. Alexa set the Glock on the table to read the gift tag.

"Are the flowers from the interior designer? You'd think she'd leave you flowers. After all, you must've paid her a bucket of money for the work she had to do in here," Winnie said.

Alexa fingered the tag, then let it drop away. "No, they're from my ex-husband, Dennis."

Winnie turned all the way around to find a long whitewashed bookcase filled with books and trinkets along the back wall. "Ah, what a lovely bookcase. And I see you do a bit of reading."

Alexa was already heading for the kitchen across from the living room. Lydia had carried the country French whitewashed style throughout these rooms. The cabinetry and the huge island that separated the living room from the kitchen featured black granite countertops with glittery golden specs throughout.

Suddenly, Winnie let out another gasp. "Well, would ya look at this!" She hurried into the kitchen to the third window. She gently ran her hand over an old window etched in a black and white design. Alexa didn't remember Lydia mentioning the window. She must've left it behind as a surprise. It was breathtaking. The etching depicted a man and a woman standing near a trough giving water to a workhorse. Great detail was observed in the fields and barn in the background. "This window was made by me grandfather back in Ireland. I'd have thought this would have been long gone."

"It's beautiful, Winnie. I'm glad Lydia left it here."

Winnie ran her fingers over the glass. "It's a treasure." She turned. "Your kitchen is—" She gasped, only this wasn't at all like the first. This gasp was of surprise. "Good Lord in the morning, it's Gar—oh, no, it couldn't be."

Alexa whirled around to see what Winnie was gaping at, a big, beautiful, white cat sitting on the far end of island. Her fluffy tail curled around her body. Her gorgeous blue eyes studied them as if they were intruding upon *her* domain. The afternoon sun shining through the window glinted off her rhinestone collar and silver name tag dangling from it. Alexa drew her right hand to her chest. "How did that cat get in here?" She took a swift step toward the island, but the cat spun, then bounded from the countertop. Alexa rushed around the island to try to catch the kitty, but it wasn't there. Winnie tossed Alexa's cell phone on the counter, then came around the other side, but no cat could be found. Alexa's questioning gaze met Winnie's. "Where did it go? I have to find it and get it out of the apartment. I'm horribly allergic to cats. I can't imagine where it came from."

Winnie took her by the arm. "Come now, let's have a seat. If we're calm, she may come out of hiding. Besides, I think we found the culprit who's making all the noise, and me feet are beggin' to test the comfort level of these chairs."

"Oh, I'm sorry. Yes, let's sit." They each took a seat. "I'm intrigued, Winnie. Tell me more about this Bobby Starr character. Why did he have so many wives?"

"Bobby was a handsome man, and that was his biggest problem. Women liked Bobby, and Bobby *loved* women. Problem was, once he got a woman, he was on to the next, and I don't think they liked that too much.

Although, I have to say, he was a nice man. I liked Bobby. Then again, I was just a lass. Sometimes, he would pull up a barstool and a beer and help me with me homework. He was good with figures." She chuckled, Alexa was certain, at a memory. "One time, he was helping me with me math when this woman came marchin' into the pub. Oh, she was as mad as a wet hen. Well, she walked right up to Bobby, grabbed his beer, said something I did not understand, dumped it over his head, and marched right out of the pub just as quick as ya please."

Alexa laughed out loud. "Oh, no! Was she one of his wives?"

"I don't know who she was. Anyway, later while me homework was dryin' on the radiator..." She pointed to a place where a radiator evidently once stood. "I asked me mother why the woman would do such a thing. She said it wasn't the first time she'd witnessed a woman takin' her frustrations out on Bobby, and she doubted it would be the last." Winnie sagged deeper into the chair, contemplatively.

Alexa said, "I wish that cat would come out of hiding. Although, I'm not wheezing and my face isn't swelling. So, that's a good thing." She could see that Winnie hadn't heard her comment. The old Irish woman was somewhere else. Most likely, somewhere that no longer existed. "A penny for your thoughts."

Winnie smiled. "Ah, I don't think they're worth that much. But if you really want to know, I'm thinking about that cat. She sure does remind me of Garbo."

"Garbo? As in the old silent movie star, Greta Garbo?"

"The *feline* version. Garbo was Bobby's second wife's cat. She looked just like the cat we saw. Same shiny collar, same silver name tag, and the same beautiful blue eyes. After Cora Lee...after her death, Bobby asked if I'd take care of Garbo. He was a detective, one of those private eye types, and he didn't have time to take care of a cat. Little girls love cats. Especially one as beautiful as Garbo. She was me best friend for a very long time. I've got the funniest feeling about that cat, but it couldn't be..." Winnie pushed up from the chair to shuffle across the room and into the kitchen.

"I should think not," Alexa confirmed with great confidence.

Winnie opened the whitewashed cabinet door to reveal the bottle of Jameson, the shot glasses, and the cake inside the car of the dumbwaiter. She grabbed up the bottle and glasses, set them on the counter, then poured whiskey into one of the glasses. She turned to face Alexa and raised the glass. "May your friends respect you, trouble neglect you, the angels protect you, and heaven accept—" She stopped. Her eyes grew wide and her face pale.

"Accept what?" Alexa slid to the end of her chair. "Winnie...are you okay?"

Winnie's voice shook. "I'm not believing what me eyes are tellin' me. It's...it's Bobby Starr, himself!" She tossed the whiskey back, then with shaking hands grabbed the bottle to pour another.

"What?" Alexa jerked from her seat, spinning around to find a man standing in the archway of her living room.

Chapter Three

Who's Bobby Starr?

Alexa grappled for her gun lying on the coffee table, and then pointed it directly at the man leaning against the arch. "Don't move, and don't underestimate the situation. I *will* shoot."

The right side of the man's lips hitched. Alexa was taken aback. The man was very handsome. His thick nest of dark hair was cut close. His brown eyes were the color of rich, dark chocolate. His strong jawline eased down into a cleft chin, as if he'd leaned it against a big ring for too long. He was tall, broad shouldered, and his clothing was sharp and crisp, yet not of today's fashion. He wore a gray suit jacket, white shirt, wide gray tie, and high-waisted trousers, cuffed. In his hands he held...was that a black fedora?

Letting the fedora fall to the floor, he raised his hands in surrender. His boyish grin never waned, hovering somewhere between diffident and appealing. "I give up, darlin', but shooting me won't change anything. The bullet will travel right through me into one of these really nice walls. I'd hate to see ya damage all this work on me."

Winnie's voice shivered. "Lordy, Lordy..." She raised yet another glass of whiskey. "Here's to the health of your enemies' enemies." She gulped the drink down.

"Wow, and what a great job that redhead did with this place. It's *never* looked like this. Love what you did with my apartment. It's a little feminine for my tastes, but it's nice. And a private bathroom. Wow, that would've been fantastic." His glance slid to Winnie. "Isn't that right, Mrs. Mulaney?"

Winnie's eyes grew wide; she took in a tiny gasp. "What did you call me?"

"Mrs. Mulaney...Mrs. Molly Mulaney?" Now there was a question in his tone.

"I'll have you know not a drop of whiskey ever breached me mother's lips, *Mr.* Bobby Starr."

Bobby's eyes narrowed. He studied the edgy woman standing in the kitchen. "I recognize the accent...Maggie? No...it couldn't be...*Winnie*?" Clearly the man was taken aback. "Why, you were just..." He lowered his right arm from the air down close to his hip. "You were just a little tyke. You look so...so..."

"*Old.* Old is the word you're lookin' for, Bobby. You've been gone a long time, and I can't say I'm that happy to see you."

Bobby shifted his gaze back to Alexa. "I think we've established that I'm a ghost. So, can I put my hands down? They're getting really tired."

Reluctantly, Alexa nodded, but kept the gun trained on the man, or ghost. She wasn't absolutely convinced.

"Whatever. What are you doing in my apartment?" Alexa asked. Her tone was tight.

"This may be hard for you to understand, but I'm trying to get a position on the Guardian Angel Squad. It's a very prestigious group of angels. But to get on the squad you have to qualify."

"Is that a fact? And how would one *qualify* to become a guardian angel?" Alexa asked.

"Usually, by setting something straight you failed to do when you were still living."

"This is just crazy," Alexa muttered.

"Peter said he'd find someone to help me fulfill my qualifications. My guess is that someone is you, Mrs. Owl."

Lowering the gun to her side, Alexa shook her head. "Peter, *who*?"

Bobby and Winnie exchanged looks. "You know..." He pointed a timid finger toward the ceiling. "Peter, as in *Saint* Peter, Saint Pete, as we angels like to call him." Alexa narrowed her eyes in complete bewilderment. He snorted. "You're not Catholic, are you?"

"She's not Catholic nor Irish," Winnie put in. She set the shot glass on the counter, then made her way over to stand next to Alexa.

"What's *that* got to with anything? Are you telling me there's really a Saint Pete? *The* Saint Pete who stands at the pearly gates and admits people into heaven or sends them to h—I mean, you-know-where?"

Bobby waved a flippant hand. "I don't think he has that much power, but yes, he does exist, and he's a *very* busy angel. He greets the new arrivals, shows them

23

around, hands out assignments to the squad, but what really keeps him busy is keeping the cats off the Lord's throne. I had no idea that would be such a problem, yet there he is shooing them several times a day."

"That's just insane," Alexa said.

Bobby shrugged. "Peter can be a little eccentric at times."

"Eccentric...that's what I said, eccentric." Feeling exasperated, Alexa turned to Winnie to whisper, "I'm sorry, should I be listening to this guy's load of crap or should I be calling the police?"

Winnie lifted a shoulder, then let it drop. "He is who he says he is. I'll give him that. The man's been dead and gone for a *long* time." She leaned in close to whisper, "Me father thought for sure he'd die in his bed at ninety-five at the hands of a jealous husband, but I fear it was a bit sooner than that."

"So, you're confirming that this man *is* a ghost?"

"I'm afraid I am. But I'm that much more afraid of what he's doing here."

Alexa took in a braced breath, placing the gun on the coffee table. "Okay, Mr. Starr. Just exactly why are you here?"

"I was hoping, rather, *Saint Pete* was hoping you'd help me get qualified for the squad," Bobby explained. He plucked the fedora from the floor, set it on the kitchen counter, then proceeded to pour himself a shot. His movements were as smooth as Astaire's.

"Do you have any idea how much I *don't* want to do that?" Alexa said. She shrugged. "I don't even know you."

"We'd get to know each other better."

"Oh, by the way, that's another thing I'm not interested in," Alexa pointed out, concisely.

He tossed back the shot, winced, then replied, "Ah, c'mon, Mrs. Owl, aren't you even the slightest bit curious what Pete requires me to do?" He pitched her a sexy smirk.

She was beginning to understand what Winnie was talking about. He was a lady's man, a player, or rather, he *used* to be a player. He was the type of man Alexa enjoyed looking at but never got involved with. "Okay, I'll bite. What is it that *Saint Pete* requires you to do to join this prestigious *squad*?"

"I have to resolve three of the five murders I left unsolved at my passing."

Alexa blinked back. "*Five* murders? You left *five murders* unsolved? I thought you were a detective."

"A private investigator. And I didn't say I was a *good* one."

"That certainly goes without saying," Alexa scoffed. She took in a calming breath. "Look, Mr. Starr, If you need a new suit made for a special occasion, I'm your girl. If your wife should need a gown made for a dinner party, call me. If your little girl needs a dress for her first Holy Communion, make an appointment. But I don't know *anything* about solving murders. I think Saint Pete has sent you to the wrong address. Perhaps you should look up Angela Lansbury, I think she's still alive. She's very good at figuring these kinds of things out."

"I just love her," Winnie put in.

"Saint Pete doesn't make mistakes, Mrs. Owl. Although, I think letting so many cats into heaven may have been a...well...let's call it an *oversight* on his part."

"Just for the sake of knowin', whose murder do you have to solve?" Winnie inquired.

"Pete said he'd assign one at a time." Bobby reached inside his jacket and pulled out a scroll tied up with a gold ribbon. He studied the scroll for a moment, then strode across the room to hand it to Winnie. "I haven't found the courage to open it. Go ahead, Winnie, have a look-see."

Winnie exchanged a wary glance with Alexa, then tentatively slipped the scroll from his hand. With shaking fingers, she removed the tie, then unfurled the paper. Cupping her hand over her mouth, she let out a gasp. Sliding her hand down to her throat, she murmured, "Good Lord in heaven...Cora Lee. It says here you must solve her murder by the eighteenth of this month. That's *July 18th*, Bobby." She made a quick attempt to return the scroll to Bobby. Just then, it curled up and disappeared in midair. Letting out a tiny yelp, Winnie flinched.

Bobby's face pinched in despair.

"This is the *second* time I've heard this woman's name today. Who is Cora Lee?" Alexa asked.

"She was my third wife," Bobby said.

"Are you sure? I thought Cora Lee was your *second* wife," Winnie interjected.

"Just exactly how many wives have you had, Mr. Starr?" Alexa asked, succinctly.

He ticked them off on his fingers. "Well, let me see now...my first wife was Catherine. About two years later, I married...Cora Lee. Yeah, that's right, she *was* the second. She was a singer at the Lazy Hound on Friday nights, and then there was Catherine—"

"You already mentioned Catherine."

"No, this was a *different* Catherine. Then I married, Venetia." He pumped his eyebrows. "She was an *exotic* dancer." Alexa rolled her eyes. "And then my last wife's name was Katherine—with a K."

Alexa's jaw slacked. She managed, "You had *three* wives named Catherine?"

Bobby scrubbed his fingers over his jaw. "It must've been a very popular name back in the twenties."

Alexa sagged into the nearest chair to absorb what Bobby had just told her. "You were like Henry the 8th. Three out of Henry's six wives were named Catherine." Her eyes widened. "You weren't *like* Henry the 8th, were you?"

"I didn't have them *beheaded*, if that's what you mean. Trust me, if anyone wanted anyone beheaded, it was the other way around."

"Imagine my surprise." Without warning, Alexa had a sudden feeling of empathy for the ghost. He wanted to become a guardian angel. Evidently that meant he wanted to help people in trouble here, on Earth. Winnie had mentioned that he was a nice man when he was alive. He'd helped her with her homework. How bad could he have been if he was willing to give up a little time to help a child with their homework? He'd been sent to her for help. Alexa wasn't exactly sure what that meant, but she had always been a believer that people are brought together for a reason—not by accident. She dragged her gaze to meet Bobby's. "Let me sleep on this, Mr. Starr. I'll give you my answer tom—Monday."

Bobby strolled to the counter, picked up the fedora,

and placed it on his head. "Until Monday, then, Mrs. Owl." With a tip of his hat, he vanished.

Letting out the breath she'd been holding, Alexa plopped back against the chair. Winnie sank into the chair across from her, leaned her head back, and closed her eyes. The silence stretched for several minutes, both women trying to grasp what had just occurred. Alexa was surprised at how tired her voice sounded when she asked, "Winnie…is now a good time to ask if you'd be interested in a bookkeeping position at my shop?"

"I was wonderin' what was takin' you so long to ask. Why do you think I showed up here today? To drink too much whiskey and bump into an old friend, a very old, *dead* friend?"

Alexa chuckled. She really liked Winnie. She was a straight-shooter.

"Then again, what if you don't like me work? Or what if I don't like the situation? I mean, you've already got dead people showin' up at your place of business," Winnie pointed out.

"Not my place of business. My apartment. Tell ya what, let's give it a month's trial. If I don't like your work, or you don't like my situations, we'll call it quits. No hard feelings. Deal?"

Winnie sat for a moment, contemplating, and then she smiled. "Deal. I'd suggest we drink to it, but I think I've hit me limit for one day."

"Or maybe you've run out of toasts?"

"Oh, I never run out of those."

ALEXA TUGGED THE BAND that held her hair atop her head, allowing silky tresses to spill about her shoulders. Through the long window of the shop's door, she watched Winnie steer her bright orange Volkswagen Beetle into traffic. It had been a long day. It had been an unbelievable day. When she'd pulled up and parked in front of her new shop, Alexa had no idea what lay in wait for her. Hitting the pothole and seeing the rude man in the red Jaguar seemed like yesterday rather than a few hours ago. She scrubbed her fingers across her forehead. What day was it again? Friday, it was Friday. She told Bobby she'd have a decision on whether she'd assist in solving his second wife's murder on Monday. And she was completely baffled how she could assist him at all.

Fatigue washing over her, she turned the deadbolt into the locked position, then leaned against the door for a moment. A dark purple hue filtered through the etched windows into the shop. Dusk was falling over the city. Grabbing up the case that held her laptop she'd left near the door, she strolled through her shop, savoring the beauty and the new prospects this new business, new location, offered. After climbing halfway up the staircase, she turned to take one last look before retiring for the evening. Yes, this is exactly the shop she'd envisioned.

She climbed the rest of the stairs and stepped into her apartment, closing and locking the door. A twist of apprehension shuddered through her stomach. It might be a little harder to settle into the apartment than the shop. After all, she'd been visited by a ghost in her new home— not something she was prepared for. Who could prepare for a ghost appearing in your new apartment the very first day? Worse, a ghost with an agenda?

Speaking of agendas, she needed to open her laptop and see what appointments she had for Monday. She'd hired a marketing company to promote the new shop and take appointments. She'd received a text message earlier in the day informing her they'd secured several new clients and appointments for Monday. She had also contacted an employment agency in hopes of finding an assistant, a bookkeeper, and a salesperson. She wanted to check her email to see if she needed to schedule interviews.

Alexa crossed the living room to a French provincial desk stationed in the far corner. Lydia wanted to whitewash the desk to match the rest of the furnishings. The desk was an antique that had belonged to her mother, and Alexa felt it would compromise the desk's integrity. So, her favorite piece of furniture remained a rich cherry finish; it made for a lovely accent piece. She plopped the case on the desk, slid out the laptop, tossed the case to the floor, and opened the computer. While waiting for the Wi-Fi to connect, she fetched her cell phone from the coffee table. That's when her eyes fell upon the floral arrangement Dennis had sent. Earlier, she'd given the note attached to the arrangement a quick once-over, then simply disregarded it. Now, she was actually seeing the bright yellow tea roses accentuated with delightful daisies all gathered in a large, yellow, happy-face mug. It was very nice. Something she would expect from Dennis. Alexa plucked the note from the plastic holder.

Dear Lexi, I wish you the best of luck with your new shop. All my love, Dennis

A svelte smile crossed her lips. They had love at one time, she and Dennis, but time had pulled them far apart. His business. Her business. No time for them. No time for love. Heck, no time for dinner at the same table. They had drifted too far. And so, they ended their eleven-year partnership—that's what it had turned into, a partnership, not a marriage. The divorce was amicable. No harsh words. No cryptic love affairs to discover. No bitterness. For that, she was most thankful.

She stuck the note back into the holder and returned to the desk. She pulled out the chair and sat. The search engine had appeared on the screen, awaiting her command. Good. The Wi-Fi was up and running without a hitch. Her fingers hovered over the keyboard. She had every intention of checking her email, but instead of pressing the little envelope icon she typed *Cora Lee Starr, death.*

Because the woman had died, or actually, in this case, had been murdered before the internet was invented, there was no instant information. Instead, the engine directed her to a site called Find a Death. The site's description boasted thousands of obituaries and news clippings dating back as far as 1900. Cool. She clicked on the link and typed in the same request. Still, there was very little information available on Cora Lee's death. However, her obituary was listed along with a photograph. She was quite lovely. No surprise. Alexa doubted Bobby Starr would be interested in anything less than a beauty. And there were two articles listed about her death, one in the *Pittsburgh Daily Times*, and another in the *Pittsburgh Post-Gazette.*

Okay, first things first, Alexa supposed. Reading the obituary seemed like a good place to begin. If nothing else, the obit would give a summary of her life and perhaps her demise. Alexa wasn't sure she was quite ready to jump into the dirty details just yet. She slid the cursor over the obit, then, with a tight knot in her stomach, she clicked on the link, and the obituary with a photograph of Cora Lee Baker-Starr filled the screen. The photograph was a professional shot: Cora Lee was posed looking over her right shoulder into the camera. A pretty blonde, fair-skinned woman with long eyelashes and a heart-shaped face. She wore a string of pearls around her neck and what appeared to be a dark-colored angora sweater. Alexa set to reading the epitaph...

Cora Lee Baker-Starr died unexpectedly on July 18, 1953. She was born October 2, 1925, in McKees Rocks, Pennsylvania. Daughter of Frank and Anna Baker. Wife of Detective Robert Starr. She was employed by Sears and Roebuck Company, East Liberty. She also was a singer at the Lazy Hound Pub, Penn Avenue. Cora Lee is survived by her husband, Robert Starr, father, Frank Baker, mother, Anna Baker, and sister, Barbara Newman. Preceded in death by her brother, George Baker. Funeral services will be held at Gilson Funeral Home, East Liberty, at 10 A.M. July 24th. Interment will be at St. Peter's Cemetery, Lemington Avenue.

The obituary was short, sweet, and contained no relevant information about how Cora Lee died. What did she expect? It was an obituary, not a newspaper article. Then again, the list of family members might prove useful. She opened the middle drawer of the desk, fished out a note-pad and pen, then jotted the names down. She closed the link, then moved on to the *Pittsburgh Daily Times*'s coverage of Bobby's second wife's death, dated July 19, 1953. The headline read: "Detective's Wife Found Dead."

In the late evening of Friday, July 18th, Private Investigator Robert Starr's wife, Cora Lee, was found dead behind the Lazy Hound Pub, Penn Avenue. Mrs. Starr was a singer at the Lazy Hound on Friday nights. She left the bar out the back door after her performance at approximately 10:30 P.M. to meet Detective Starr at a dinner party. Her body was discovered among the trash cans behind the bar by Wynona Mulaney when she was taking out the evening trash. Wynona is the daughter of Brian Mulaney, who is the proprietor of the Lazy Hound Pub.

The coroner indicated that Mrs. Starr had been strangled to death. An investigation is ongoing with no suspects at this time.   ~ Ray Howell/Pittsburgh Daily Times

Letting her hands fall away from the keyboard, Alexa sagged in her seat. "My God," she whispered to herself. "Winnie found Cora Lee's body. She couldn't have been more than eight or nine years old at the time. How awful."

She slapped the laptop lid closed. She'd read quite enough for the evening. Exhausted, she took up her Glock and made her way toward the bedroom. Alexa was almost certain tonight would be a restless one.

Chapter Four

Garbo

As she suspected would be the case, Alexa saw almost every hour pass during the night. She'd tossed and wrangled in her sheets with thoughts of Cora Lee's untimely demise that took place directly behind her shop. At three A.M. she whipped the blankets aside, pressed up from the mattress, and padded across the room to the window that looked out over the small parking lot behind her building. The street lamps along 25th Street lent a soft eerie glow across the six-car lot. Yesterday afternoon had been thick with humidity. A light haze hovered beneath the lamps, reminding Alexa of many an old mystery movie.

So, where had the trash cans been located back in 1953? Not particularly wild about the idea of venturing out to that lonely lot in the wee hours of the morning, she pressed her body as close as she could to the long window, then squirmed until she had a view of the right corner of the building. That's where *she* would place her cans, but was that where the Mulaneys had stationed theirs? Did Cora Lee know her attacker, or was she easy prey in a dark parking lot on a hot July night? Why did she exit the pub via the back door? Why didn't she go out the front where there would have been more people? Maybe she had a car parked in the lot.

Wait a minute. Alexa rushed to the nightstand to grab up her cell phone. She pressed the button. It was July 14th. The 18th would be the sixty-eighth anniversary of Cora Lee's murder. The scroll indicated that Bobby must solve Cora Lee's murder by the 18th—that was only *four* days away! Four days? How was she, a totally amateur gumshoe—at best—and a completely incompetent detective going to solve a case from *1953* in four days?

Impatience, or maybe it was pure panic, ripped through her. Alexa yanked open the drawer on the nightstand to retrieve her Glock. She snatched her robe lying at the foot of the bed, slipped one arm in, then came to a halt. Hold on. What was she doing? Going down to that lonely parking lot at three A.M.? Just exactly what was *that* going to accomplish? There were no trash cans. She hadn't purchased any as of yet. There was no evidence lying about waiting to be discovered. Do the math. The woman was murdered *sixty-eight* years ago. She tossed the robe onto the bed, returned the Glock to the drawer, then lay down, pulling the blanket over her. The click of the air conditioning unit turning on and the sudden whoosh of cool air permeating from the register made her flinch. She let out an aggravated grouse. Enough was enough. There was nothing she could do for Cora Lee Starr at this time, maybe never. She needed to calm down, close her eyes, and get some much-needed sleep.

THE SUN FILTERING THROUGH the curtains warmed Alexa's face. Her eyes fluttered open, and the brightness made her squint, then shade her eyes with her elbow. Around a groggy groan, she stretched her arm toward the nightstand, feeling around for her cell phone, then fumbling to pick it up. The screen announced: 8:30 A.M. Hokay, she had a ton of stuff to get done, including a bit of grocery shopping. Slowly, she pressed up from the pillow to find the white cat, supposedly known as Garbo, perched on the footboard of the bed. The feline was scrutinizing her with those hauntingly gorgeous blue eyes. The sun winked off the silver name tag gently swaying from her collar.

Without warning nor sound, Garbo jumped down from the bed. Alexa craned her neck looking for the cat. She had to wonder if the cat had become bored with the new mistress of the apartment. Then suddenly, she appeared on the chair posted near the window. The cat licked her right paw for a moment, then, after shooting Alexa a quick, dismissive glance, she leapt onto the back of the chair to stare out the window. The morning sun shone directly through the cat's body. Indeed, Garbo was translucent. She seemingly gazed in the direction Alexa had surmised the trash cans may have been located all those years ago.

Had Garbo been sitting in the window that ill-fated night in July? Had the cat witnessed the murder of her former mistress? Is that why the cat remained in the apartment? Was she waiting for justice for Cora Lee's death? If so, she'd kept watch for a very long time.

Alexa wondered if she could communicate with Garbo. She cooed, "Kitty, kitty...come here, pretty kitty." Garbo didn't budge from her station at the window. Then again, Alexa had heard cats are nothing like dogs—you can't call a cat. They are far too sophisticated for such trivial things as being summoned to their master. Regardless, Alexa gave it another go. "Garbo...pretty, pretty Garbo..." Still the cat stared out the window, ignoring her calls. Disappointed, Alexa's shoulders drooped. She'd always wanted a cat, and this cat didn't make her sneeze, wheeze, cry, swell, or turn various shades of red. Garbo was so beautiful. Alexa wanted to caress her fur, and she wondered what the cat would do if she tried. What did she have to lose? She scooched off the bed and padded to the chair, then reached out to stroke Garbo's head. The cat turned to meet her gaze, and then she was gone.

"Guess not," Alexa sighed. She slipped into the blue and white floral silk robe with blue cuffs, tying the sash around the flowing blue nightgown. Just then, her cell phone rang. She picked it up from the bed. The screen announced Natalyn La Pearle, her younger sister. Natalyn was ten years Alexa's junior. She was an afterthought baby, born late in her parents' marriage. Her mother had just turned forty when Natalyn arrived. Alexa pressed the answer button. "Good morning."

"Where are you?" Natalyn sounded annoyed, and rightly so. She'd promised to call her little sister when she arrived in the Burgh, and she hadn't. Whoops.

"I'm at my apartment."

"In *Pittsburgh*? Why didn't you call?"

"I got in later than I expected, and then…um…something happened."

"Well, I've been dying to see your shop. I've driven by several times. It looks great from the outside, but I'd love to see the inside. Are you going to be there all day?"

That was Natalyn. She talked fast, drove fast, and lived fast. Why not? She was twenty-four, amazingly beautiful, unattached, educated, with the promise of a great life ahead of her. Mom and Dad had seen to that before their passing. Alexa's father, Sam La Pearle, passed away four years ago of a massive heart attack, and her mother, Jennifer, last spring, breast cancer.

Natalyn lived in an upscale apartment complex on Fifth Avenue in Oakland across from the Mansions on Fifth, a swanky convention, wedding, or banquet venue. Her apartment was spacious and had a private parking garage that included a valet. Yeah, everything was always coming up roses for Natalyn La Pearle.

"Okay," Natalyn began. "I'll be over around three. That should give you enough time to do a few things. And I'll help you with anything you need from there. Sound good?"

Not really, but it would be good to spend time with her sister, with family. Alexa said, "Three it is."

"Look, Lexi, I know you've been preoccupied with the divorce, selling one shop and setting up another, and of course, the move, but…we've really got to get Mom and Dad's house on the market. Yes, we had the estate auction, and got rid of most of the furniture and stuff, but the house has been sitting empty for over a year now… it's time."

A beleaguered sigh escaped her before Alexa could call it back. Natalyn was right. Some things are hard to let go of. Mom and Dad's house...*home,* was one of those things. She and her younger sister were raised by two wonderful people in a big, roomy old house in Mount Lebanon. The house was worth well over eight hundred grand, but it was *their* house. It was home. Now, it was time for it to become someone else's home. Some other family would carve the Thanksgiving turkey in the elegant dining room. Some other little girl would occupy her bedroom. Some other family would decorate a Christmas tree in that big, comfy living room, or sing carols along with Bing Crosby, while baking Christmas cookies in the warmth of the kitchen. No matter how she or Natalyn felt...it was time to let go. Let go of the *house,* not Mom or Dad or the memories they'd been blessed with.

"Lexi..."

Her sister's gentle nudge broke through her muse. Raking her fingers through her bed-tossed tresses, she replied, "Yes, I agree. It's time. See you at three. And Nat...I've missed you."

"I've missed you too. See you soon." With that, she disconnected the call.

Alexa had sent Lydia some extra money to do a little grocery shopping for her so when she arrived, she wouldn't be totally without food. She opened the fridge to find eggs, margarine, skim milk, coffee, French vanilla creamer, a package of bagels, and a loaf of bread. Good. Her eyes slid to the counter where the leftover chocolate cake Winnie baked sat. Not exactly breakfast food, but it sure was delish. Feeling a tug of guilt before she'd even committed the crime, she opted for a bagel and coffee. She retrieved the toaster from atop the fridge, stuffed a bagel inside, then proceeded to make coffee in the machine on the counter. Lydia had been a dream—more helpful than any designer she could have hoped for, and she'd never actually met the woman. As the coffee brewed and the bagel toasted, Alexa explored the drawers and cabinets. She needed to become familiar with where things had been placed, and maybe move things around a bit. She was looking through the cabinets near the sink, ah, there were the coffee mugs. As she plucked a mug from the shelf, she heard a soft *meow*.

She turned to find Garbo sitting on the far corner of the island. Those penetrating blue eyes locked on Alexa. Was she hungry? How could that be? Garbo was a ghost cat. Then again, Bobby did have a drink of whiskey when he was in the apartment yesterday. If Garbo was hungry, when was the last time she'd eaten? No one had occupied the apartment for...who knows how long. Unless, the construction crew or Lydia had been feeding her. If so, did that mean anyone could see Garbo or just her? Ghost stuff was really confusing, and it was starting to get to her.

The cat let out another *meow*, then jumped down from the island, only this time she didn't disappear. She slinked toward the hallway, then paused at the arch to glance over her shoulder at Alexa as if to say, Well, human, aren't you going to follow me? Garbo didn't linger very long before she continued out of the room. Alexa hurried to the archway to see if she was still there or if she'd vanished, as had been her practice. But there she was, sauntering along until she reached the threshold of the bedroom. She hesitated again to see if the dumb human was trailing along. The moment Alexa stepped forward, Garbo continued into the room.

Did she want to be followed or was this some kind of cat prank? Alexa wished Winnie were here. She was familiar with the cat. Oh, come now, what did it matter what the cat's intentions were? Ghost or no, it was a cat. Alexa made her way into the bedroom to find Garbo resting on the chair, gazing out the window as she had earlier in the morning.

A strange feeling coiled through Alexa. It was close to the anniversary of Cora Lee's death. Was Garbo expecting something to happen? Was she anticipating her former mistress to make some kind of spectral visit? She hoped not. One man-ghost and one cat-ghost were plenty as far as Alexa was concerned.

Curiosity and the cat were getting the better of her—not necessarily a good combination. As the old wives' tale suggested, curiosity killed the cat. Alexa decided it was time to check out the parking lot behind the shop. She'd left her Lexus parked out front overnight. Perhaps she'd take this opportunity to move the vehicle to the lot and have a look around in the meantime. Of course, she didn't expect to find anything of pertinence, but at least she would be familiar with the area. It seemed like a very detective thing to do, anyway.

She scooped up the clothes she'd worn yesterday from the floor, changed, tossing the robe and nightgown onto the bed, pressed into her flip-flops, then proceeded to the kitchen to pour a cup of coffee and grab the keys from her purse. Before heading downstairs, she leaned into the bedroom to see if Garbo was still sitting at her post. Indeed, the cat hadn't moved. She was practicing a steady surveillance.

Alexa unlocked the door to step out of her apartment, then jogged down the staircase, across the shop, unlocked the front door, and out onto the sidewalk. The morning sun was brilliant and unforgiving. The heat was already stifling and the Strip was already abuzz with Saturday morning shoppers vying for parking spots. She was certain the moment she pulled out of her spot it would be snatched up immediately. She hopped into the car, pressed the ignition switch, signaled her intent to merge with traffic, and sure enough, a white SUV turned on their signal, indicating they were pulling into her spot. *Thump, thump-thump.* The SUV hit the pothole; there was just no missing it. Alexa rolled the Lexus into traffic and made the immediate right-hand turn onto 25th Street, and by the time she was steering the Lexus into her parking lot there were only two spots left. She would have to put a sign up designating this was a private lot; otherwise, her Saturday customers would struggle to park close to the shop.

Alexa peered up at her bedroom window through the windshield. Yep, she could see Garbo as plain as day. She slid from the vehicle at the same time a middle-aged woman was getting out of a Ford Escort.

"Excuse me, ma'am..." The woman turned, looking her up and down. She probably appeared a bit disheveled. She hadn't even bothered to wash her face or run a brush through her hair.

"Yes?" the woman said, her tone just this side of terrified.

Alexa pointed toward the window. "Do you see a white cat in that window?"

The woman took a half step backward as she followed the upward direction of the young woman's finger. Her narrowed eyes flicked toward the peculiar woman. Her lip crinkled just a bit. Her head cocked to one side. "Do *you* see a cat in the window?" Well, that settled it. The woman thought she was a complete nutcase, because obviously she could *not* see Garbo perched on the chair through the window.

Before Alexa could reply, the woman held up a halting hand. "Look, I just want to go to the fish market. So, please, just leave me alone." She spun on her heels to hurry away, her Ford letting out a *beep beep* as she scampered from the lot. She glanced anxiously over her shoulder every so often to make sure the crazy woman who saw invisible cats in windows wasn't chasing after her. Alexa couldn't really blame her. In truth, *she* was starting to feel like a crazy woman who saw invisible cats.

AFTER ALEXA CHANGED into fresh clothes, put on a full-length bib apron, and pulled her hair up, she spent the rest of morning in the back room. She uncrated her sewing machines, took inventory of the bolts and bolts of fabric, colorful spools of thread, and boxes of needles that had been delivered over the past week. She was pleased with all her equipment and required inventory, including her mom's old mangle that Alexa still used to press clothes. The mangle was big and bulky, but it did a better job than modern-day steamers Now, she simply had to get it all organized by Monday.

Alexa had just propped the final bolt of fabric, a gorgeous gold crystal organza, onto the shelving unit when an obvious thought crossed her mind: if Bobby Starr was deceased and residing in heaven, and Cora Lee was in heaven, why on earth couldn't he simply ask the woman who had killed her and why? This would be an immediate inquiry of Mr. Starr the moment he returned looking for his answer. Then again, the ability to just ask the woman who killed her would be way too easy a challenge or *requirement* to gain acceptance into the "squad." Then again, maybe that was the whole idea. Perhaps *Pete* expected Bobby to find the easiest answer to difficult problems so he could help people as quickly as possible. She rubbed her lower back. Something to seriously consider.

Just then, there was a loud buzzing. The sound was the alarm warning her that someone had entered the front door of the shop. Alexa glanced up at the big, round clock on the wall stationed above the door that led back onto the main floor of the shop. It was five minutes of three. Natalyn. Alexa's younger sister may live on the fast side of life, but God bless the girl, she was a stickler for punctuality.

She could hear Natalyn calling, "Lex...Lex..."

She untied the apron, pulled it over her head, and tossed it over one of the sewing machines. Quickly, she kicked off her flip-flops and pressed into a pair of sparkly slip-on shoes. She brushed her hands over her faded jeans and smoothed the short-sleeved V-neck top with a dainty lace inset across the hem. She pulled the tie from her hair, shook it a bit, then hurried through the door to greet her sister. Alexa opened her arms wide. "There she is, Miss Punctuality."

Chuckling, Natalyn waved a flippant hand. "Eh, it's a curse."

A nanosecond later, Garbo slinked through the shop, jumped up on the bar, then proceeded to clean her paws. She'd abandoned her post at the bedroom window. Was she checking on Alexa, or was she playing with her sanity? She'd heard cats could be like that.

"The shop is fabulous. Your designer did a wonderful job. Are you satisfied with her work? I can't imagine you're not. Lex...Lex..."

Realizing Natalyn had been talking to her, Alexa blinked back into the moment. "What? Oh, yes, Lydia did a great job. Everything is just as I wanted it. The apartment too. By the way, do you see a cat anywhere in here?"

"A cat?" Natalyn turned in a small circle, searching the expanse of the room. "No. You don't have a cat, do you? I thought you were allergic."

"No, I don't *own* a cat." She shot a look at Garbo, who seemed completely bored with the humans in *her* domain. Alexa muttered under her breath, "At least, I didn't *think* I did."

"You are so *weird*," Natalyn snorted.

"Weird is my super power," Alexa playfully pointed out. "Hey, I'm done working around here for the day. How about we grab something to eat and maybe a glass of wine or two?"

"Sounds good, but...please don't get mad...I've made arrangements to meet a real estate agent at the house in about a half hour." Wincing, Natalyn's body crinkled up like she was anticipating an explosion.

"Half hour? With the Saturday traffic, we'll have just enough time to get there. I'll show you the apartment when we get back. I'll pay for dinner. You pay for the wine.

Smiling, Natalyn looked relieved. "Sounds like a plan. I'll drive."

WHEN ONE APPROACHES MIDDLE-AGE, one is far more comfortable with driving according to the speed limit, or at the very least, within five miles of the speed limit. In Natalyn's world, the number on the rectangular white sign displayed along the highway was more of a suggestion than a law. By the time they arrived at the greystone house on Hoodridge Drive, Alexa was shocked her right foot hadn't gone straight through the floor of the white Toyota Supra. She had little recollection of passing through the Fort Pitt Tunnel, and she was quite certain she'd never reached the top of Green Tree Hill before light or sound could catch up. Natalyn chatted and joked and giggled the entire trip, all while using hand motions. Alexa hadn't heard one thing she said. She was far too busy trying to survive the ride.

Natalyn slowed the sports car down to a cool thirty-five before whipping into the driveway, then coming to a blessed stop within inches of the garage doors. "Looks like we beat the real estate agent," Natalyn said, as the seat belt recoiled over her left shoulder with a *snap*.

Alexa raked her fingers through her hair. "Looks like we arrived alive. Barely." Trying to reconcile with her nerves, she unhooked the seat belt, then slowly climbed out of the car just as a zero-turn mower came around the corner of the house next door, Mr. and Mrs. Slater's home.

Natalyn waved at the man driving the mower. His smile was pleasant and his mirrored aviator glasses reflected the sports car. His blue T-shirt was wet with sweat, clinging to his sculpted chest. His long, muscled legs poured out of a pair of jeans shorts, and he wore a pair of old, beat-up Nikes. He turned the mower off, then dismounted and walked toward them. The sun kissed droplets of sweat clinging to the tips of the curls in his dark hair. Alexa's pulse hitched a bit.

Alexa leaned close to her sister. "Who is that?"

"You don't remember Cliff Slater? He said he graduated high school with you."

"I remember Cliff Slater. I just don't remember *that version* of Cliff Slater."

"He's been cutting the grass for the past year. He cuts his parents' yard, so, he said it wasn't a problem to cut ours."

Cliff approached the girls. "Hi, I just finished your yard about a half hour ago. The window-washer stopped by just before you pulled in. He wanted to know if you wanted the windows washed." He reached into his hip pocket and pulled out a business card. "He left his card." He pushed his sunglasses from his face to his head, then extended the card out toward Alexa. "Alexa La Pearle. Haven't seen you in years."

She was staring. He was…stunning. She didn't remember the man being so…gorgeous. She cleared her throat. "I've been…away, but I'm back in the area now."

His hazel eyes flicked to her hand, her left hand, then, seeming to be pleased at the absence of a ring, his gaze returned to hers. "I'm glad to hear that. Maybe I'll see more of you…now that you're back in town. Natalyn told me you bought a shop in the Strip." The sound of a car pulling into the drive caused them to look up. "You've got company. I'll get out of your way. Hey, it was good to see you." With that, he made his way across the driveway toward the mower.

Natalyn nudged Alexa with her elbow. "I think he was trying to pick you up."

Alexa's lips curled as she watched Cliff climb back onto the mower. "Mm, and I think I was letting him."

As he turned to switch on the tractor, he looked up and tossed her a wink and a smile, then dropped the sunglasses back over his eyes.

Well, how about that. Alexa favored him with the same.

Chapter Five

Good Company—Bad Timing

Alexa was a bit disappointed in the employment agency she'd hired. They hadn't sent her any possible hires for her shop. Good thing she wasn't in a terrible rush. In the agency's defense, it was probably a challenge to find a qualified seamstress or tailor these days. Hopefully, one would pop up soon. On the other hand, the marketing company who'd spent the last three weeks promoting her shop and taking appointments had paid off. She had three appointments for tomorrow and several more during the week.

9 A.M.: Hayden Mann, a news anchor from one of the main Pittsburgh channels. He needed a lightweight, casual suit for his daughter's wedding in late August, which was taking place in the Bahamas. Alexa was hoping this particular client would usher her shop into more commerce from the television station. Local celebrities were always good for business.

11 A.M.: Fiona Quinn, who would be bringing a

wedding dress she'd purchased in for alterations. No wedding date was given for this client.

1 P.M.: Murielle Baker required a mother-of-the-bride style dress for a late September wedding. Preferably in a soft shade of rose.

Three well spread out Monday appointments was a perfect scenario, giving her an opportunity to ease into a schedule. She had no doubt there would be walk-in clients as the week progressed. Alexa's only big concern was, when would Bobby Starr decide to make his appearance, and what would that look like this time around?

She'd just finished the final touches on the wedding jewelry display on the glass shelves behind the bar when the front door buzzer sang out. Because she'd planned for the shop to be closed on Sundays, she'd left the door locked. Maybe Natalyn had dropped by again. Alexa made her way to the window to peer out, and much to her surprise and delight, Cliff Slater was standing outside the door. There it was again, that little hitch in her pulse. She fluffed her hair with her fingers while trotting toward the door, then stopped to gathered her composure. After all, she didn't want him to know what her pulse was doing. She took a deep breath, unlocked the door, then opened it.

"Cliff, what a nice surprise. How did you know where my shop was?"

He smiled that same sexy smile he'd tossed her yesterday. Only today he wasn't wearing old yard-work clothes; rather, he was wearing a pair of faded jeans, and a blue, short-sleeved, button-down shirt, untucked. She could see her reflection in the mirrored aviators and wished she could see his eyes—those spectacular hazel eyes. His hair was neatly combed, and she couldn't decide if she liked it better when it was damp and scruffy.

"Your sister said you had a new shop in the Strip. This is the only new establishment that I know of, and your name is Alexa...although, I didn't know your last name was Owl." He hitched his chin to the etching on the door. "Anyway, I figured this was it. I mean, that's what I do for a living, find people. I'm a police detective."

"That is so...er...rather, come in." She stepped aside to give him entry, then closed and locked the door behind him. "I'm not open on Sunday, so I'm keeping the door locked today."

"Oh, I hope I'm not interrupting—"

"No, no, not at all. I'm so glad you stopped by." She turned and extended her arm outward. "Well, this is it... my couturier shop."

He walked around, taking in the mirrors, the bar, then stepped inside the dressing rooms as well. "Wow, this is really impressive, fancy. So, you make clothing, like suits and stuff?"

"That's right. My mother used to sew all the time. She was a fantastic seamstress. She taught me. I fell in love with fabric and creating, so she taught me. And well, here I am."

"That's great. I wish you all the best with your new business."

An awkward silence lingered between them. Alexa wasn't having it. "Hey, I've got some killer chocolate cake upstairs, that's where my apartment is. Anyway, my new bookkeeper brought it for me yesterday, and it is absolutely the best. Would you like to come up and have some cake and maybe some coffee?"

Again, he flashed his pearly whites. "Sounds good." She led him up the stairs and into the apartment. They passed through the small foyer, her bedroom, and into the living room. "Wow, this is really nice. I've passed this building a million times. I would've never thought it could look like this inside."

Alexa went into the kitchen and gathered the cake on the counter. She carried it to the island, then returned to the counter to make the coffee. "Well, it didn't look anything like this when we started. It took seven months to pull it all together. I'm happy with the results. Please, have a seat." She gestured to the stools stationed at the other side of the island. Cliff sat down, and as the coffee brewed, she sliced two pieces of cake, set them on plates along with forks, then slid one across the island toward Cliff.

"Whoa. This looks like two extra hours at the gym," Cliff said. He forked a piece of the cake.

"Yeah, but trust me, it's oh, so worth it." She eased onto the stool next to him.

"Sooo, your name is Owl..."

"I'm divorced." She held up a hand. "No big story to tell. It was very amicable. In fact, the flowers on the coffee table are from him, wishing me well with the new shop."

He glanced over his shoulder at the bouquet, then said, "Amicable is good."

"I know, right?"

"Ya know, I had it bad for you in high school. In fact, I actually had some crazy moments when I almost found the guts to ask you to the prom."

Alexa chanced a quick askance glance. "Aw, you should have. I would've gone."

He lowered his fork to the plate, while pitching her a baleful look. "No, you wouldn't have."

Around a mouthful of the decadent whiskey-drenched chocolate, she chuckled, then managed, "You're right. I wouldn't have. I was too *enthralled* with Jason Van Dyne."

"Ah, yes, the big-time quarterback. I could've never competed with the likes of him."

"Probably not." She pushed up from the stool to make her way to the counter. "I wonder what ever became of him." She poured two mugs of coffee. "I thought he got a full-ride football scholarship to a big college. Hm, I just realized I've never seen him on TV playing for a team like the Steelers or Patriots or whoever." She carried the mugs to the island, setting one down in front of him, then retrieved the creamer from the fridge and a sugar bowl from the cabinet.

Cliff lifted another bite of cake to his lips. "And you won't. He's in prison." He stuffed the cake into his mouth.

Alexa set the creamer and sugar down, then gasped. "What? *No way.* What did he do?"

Cliff lifted an indifferent shoulder. "He killed his wife about three years ago. I was the lead on the case. I believe he got life."

She was about to pour creamer into her mug but stopped. "*You* solved the case?"

"That's the whole idea, isn't it?"

An opportunity to glean how-to information had just presented itself. She proceeded to pour the creamer, then plucked the lid from the sugar bowl. "Yes, of course. Sooo, how exactly do you go about solving a murder case?"

Cliff took a sip of his black coffee. "Talk to witnesses, if you're lucky enough to have any that actually cooperate. Follow leads. You know, the whole CSI–Los Angeles thing, only not nearly as sexy."

That was a matter of opinion.

The teaspoon tinkled against the mug as she stirred her coffee. "What about an old murder, a...*cold* case? How do you go about solving one of those?"

"Depending on how old the case is, those can be really tough to crack. Witnesses die or disappear altogether. Evidence gets lost in the shuffle of time. It's unfortunate, but many really old cold cases are never solved."

Movement at the archway that led to the back area of the apartment caught Alexa's eye. Bobby Starr appeared. He smiled at her. She was promptly annoyed. "What are you—" Instantly, her voice dropped away. Bobby disappeared. Cliff shot her a questioning look. She quickly conjured, "Excuse me, I need to...um...fix something." She jumped up from her seat. "I'll be right back." She hurried through the archway and into the small foyer outside her bedroom. No Bobby Starr. Where had that menacing ghost gone?

"Looking for me?" Bobby inquired. He was standing in her bedroom, sporting a most irritating smirk.

Alexa shot a quick glance over her shoulder, then marched into the bedroom. Her whisper was on the edge of way too loud. "What are you doing here? I thought, no, I *know* I told you I'd talk with you on *Monday*. In case you haven't noticed, today is *Sunday*. Now, what are you doing here?"

"I came a little early because we really don't have that much time to solve Cora's—"

"Yes, I've realized that myself, but as you saw, I have company," Alexa pointed out, concisely.

"Oh, I noticed. I thought you were married."

"Divorced."

"Oh, I'm sorry. Did he cheat on you?"

Alexa's fists drew into tight balls. "No, he didn't—that's *none* of your business!"

"You seem really upset by it. Are you sure he didn't cheat on you? Because—"

"I want you to go away, and don't come back until tomorrow, or don't come back at all. That would be just fine too!" At that moment, she noticed Bobby pointing to something over her shoulder. Dread sliced through her as sharp as any carving knife. Slowly, she turned around to find Cliff standing at the threshold of her bedroom. Cliff's eyes were as wide as a child woken from a nightmare. Alexa tried to speak, but nothing came out.

"Is everything okay in here?" Cliff asked. Cautiously, he leaned into the room, obviously looking for someone, something, anything to explain Alexa's crazy behavior.

It certainly seemed everyone was seeing Alexa's behavior as crazy of late. She choked back her rage. "Yes. Yes, everything's just fine."

"I thought I heard you talking to someone."

Alexa waved her hand as if waving away a pesky bug. "I was just talking to my...my..." she pointed to a voice-activated smart speaker on the nightstand. "Whizz Kid, you know, one of those silly smart speakers. I just reinstalled mine today, and it's been acting all...crazy, talking when I don't want it to. I heard it talking from the kitchen and came in to shut it up."

Clearly he wasn't convinced. "I've got to go. I have some things to do, and I've got an early morning tomorrow. I really enjoyed our visit. I hope we can do it again... sometime."

Alexa's heart sank. "I am so glad you stopped in to see me. I hope you'll come again, *soon.*"

He smiled, but it wasn't a *you better believe I'll be back soon* smile. It was more of a *we'll see, but probably not* smile. "Hey, good luck with your new business." He hesitated, like he simply didn't know what to say next. "See ya later." With that he turned and made his exit. She listened to his footfalls on the stairs and to the front door closing.

Her shoulders wilted. She let out a long, miserable sigh, then she heard a soft *meow*. Garbo padded across the room and jumped up on the chair to attend to her charge.

Alexa fell back onto the bed. She was beginning to wonder if her divorce was as amicable as she thought. She was beginning to think Dennis knew this place was haunted.

Chapter Six

Time is Ticking

Another restless, sleepless night. By the time Alexa had crawled from her bed at seven A.M. the bedding looked like a violent skirmish had taken place. Her mind had been overcome with thoughts of Cora Lee's murder that had taken place so many years ago. As Cliff Slater had pointed out, there might be no way of finding the killer at this late date. Cliff Slater. She'd wrestled with her sheets over the disastrous outcome of her unforeseen but delicious visit with Cliff, totally sabotaged by Bobby Starr. Oh, and how many times during the wee hours of horrid wakefulness had she punched her pillow over that scoundrel, Bobby Starr? And then, of course, the stress over tomorrow, or rather, *today* being the opening day of her new shop. Not to mention, the expected return of Bobby Starr.

One thing remained unchanged during the night: Garbo's vigilant watch over the parking lot beneath the bedroom window. At times, Alexa would lie very still, taking in the cat's solemn silhouette in the pool of golden moonlight spilling through the window. It made her heart heavy, and she wondered, if they succeeded, by some miracle, to solve Cora Lee's murder, would Garbo disappear forever? The cat was nowhere to be found this morning. Not to worry, Garbo would randomly show up during the course of the day to check on the activity in the shop.

If she was going to survive this day without a bit of sleep, Alexa was going to require that all-encompassing sustenance, caffeine. She needed to down four or five cups of joe, and then there'd be no stopping her. Dragging her arms through the armholes of her robe, and without tying the sash, she scooped up her cell phone from the nightstand, then shuffled into the kitchen to turn on the coffeemaker. She checked her messages. Winnie had texted that she would arrive around eight. The first client, Hayden Mann, was scheduled to arrive at nine. Perfect. She'd have plenty of time to show Winnie the office, go over the computer program for the shop, and have a serious chat about the details of Cora Lee's death. Of course, Winnie was just a young girl at the time, but Alexa had no doubt the woman would remember how she found Cora Lee's body. She was also counting on Winnie to remember specifics, like the location and placement of the trash cans, the position of the body, and possibly the events directly afterward. If she planned on accomplishing all that before nine, she'd better get a shower and worry about gulping coffee afterward.

IT WAS EXACTLY EIGHT O'CLOCK when Winnie pressed through the door. She was still wearing the beige orthopedic shoes, a pair of light blue slacks, and a long, oversized but well-tailored blue floral blouse with the collar flipped up. This must be a look she favored or perhaps found most comfortable. No matter, she looked well put together. Pushing the door with her elbow, Winnie lugged the red tote over her shoulder and balanced a large tray wrapped in aluminum foil on her hands.

Alexa rushed toward her. "Here, let me help you with that, Winnie. What is all this?"

"Well, it's the opening day of your new business. You've got to have cookies to offer up to your new customers. The customers at the Lazy Hound always loved me mother's Irish cream cookie balls. I was busy all day yesterday makin' them and some other cookies too."

"Irish cream?" Alexa set the tray on the end of the bar nearest the window where she had a large coffeemaker, mugs, and fixings set up. She rolled the foil back to reveal perfectly shaped chocolate balls heavily dusted with white nonpareils. The cookies looked as decadent as the cake Winnie had brought on Friday. There must've been at least six dozen on the tray. "Oh, my, Winnie, they're beautiful. You didn't have to do this—"

Winnie waved a dismissive hand. "I wanted to do it. I love to bake, and you've given me good reason to do so."

"Well, thank you so much, Winnie. Now, you said they're made with Irish cream..."

"Baileys. And plenty of it. If I'm gonna do something, I'm doin' it up right. Now, have one or two, you'll love them. They're almost better than sex if you're askin' me."

As Alexa plucked a cookie from the tray, she had to wonder if Winnie was referring to sex in the present tense or the past. She popped the little ball into her mouth. The chocolate was melt-in- your-mouth delicious, with an added explosion of Baileys Irish Cream. Alexa closed her eyes, savoring the blast of flavors dancing on her taste buds. Finally, she replied, "I agree, these cookies are almost better than sex." For her, it was definitely past tense. The two women giggled. "Are you trying to fatten me up, Winnie?"

"Ah, there are plenty of men in this world who love a voluptuous woman. Ya just don't see such things on TV. Now, where might me desk be?"

"The door at the end of bar leads into the office and a small kitchen. Your desk and the computer are all set up. Do you know how to use bookkeeping software?"

"I'm sure the computer and I will get along just fine. I haven't been retired all that long. Have ya managed to find an assistant or a salesgirl?"

"Not yet, but I'm sure I'll find at least a salesperson soon. I'm going to stick a Help Wanted sign in the front window."

"You've got plenty of other things to worry about, lass. I'll make one up and set it in the window for ya."

"Thanks, Winnie." Alexa glanced at her watch: 8:17. "Could we sit down for a minute? I'd like to talk to you about something. Can I get you a cup of coffee?"

Winnie pulled a bottle of Baileys from that enchanted red tote of hers. "Don't mind if I do. Make sure you put a generous drop of this in me coffee. It'll brighten it up a bit. And leave it out for your customers. We want to brighten their day too." She set the Baileys on the bar, then shuffled toward the French provincial sofa, stationed in the middle of the shop in front of the triple full-length mirrors. She eased onto the sofa, and as she made a few adjustments to her snowy white locks in the mirrors, she said, "I think I know what you're gonna ask me about."

"You do?" Alexa replied, as she poured a liberal drop of Baileys into Winnie's coffee and just a splash into her own.

"You're gonna ask about the night I found poor Cora Lee's lifeless body lying among the trash cans. Ooh, sometimes I still see her in me dreams. She was such a lovely woman, kind, sweet, and she sang like a bird. The customers loved to come in on Friday nights to hear Cora Lee sing." Alexa handed her a mug, then sat down on the other end of the sofa, crossing her right leg over her left. Winnie stared into her mug for a moment. "I often wonder if the murderer came to hear her sing before he *snuffed* the life out of her."

Alexa took a sip of her coffee. The Baileys really did brighten it up. "So, you think it may have been one of the regular customers?"

"I don't know. It could've been anyone."

"Tell me about the night Cora Lee died. Starting with what time she took the stage."

Around a chuckle, Winnie waved a hand. "It wasn't as fancy as all that. We didn't have a stage. On Friday night, about seven o'clock, we'd roll out an old upright piano from the back room, the same room where you're to do your sewin'. We'd set it up in the corner, there." She pointed to the far corner of the room where the bridal fitting suite was presently located. "Me father had bought an old microphone from one of the other bars, and he'd set it next to the piano. That was as fancy as it got, I'm afraid. Ah, I can still see it all sittin' there." She gazed at the corner with a sweet smile on her lips and clearly a sweeter memory in her heart.

"Would Cora Lee arrive just in time to sing or would she come in a bit early?"

"Cora Lee was a friendly, social sort, that she was. She'd come in about an hour before she was supposed to sing and lift a pint or two with friends. Then me father would go to the microphone and introduce her around nine. Me mother played the piano, and Cora Lee would sing for about an hour, take a little break, then she'd sing for a while longer. When she was done, she'd go upstairs to her and Bobby's apartment."

"You were very young at the time, Winnie. Were you allowed in the bar area?"

"Not really. I spent me Friday and Saturday nights in the kitchen washin' dishes. But I took out the trash several times a night, and me father would let me sit on the stairs right at nine o'clock so I could listen to Cora Lee sing." She chuckled. "I got an eyeful bit more on *those* nights, I can tell ya that. Me sisters, Ellie and Maggie, were old enough to serve the tables, so they were running all around. Now and then, they'd toss me a dirty look. I imagine they were wishin' they could sit and watch the show."

"So, that night, the night Cora Lee was killed, you were sent to take out the trash," Alexa confirmed. Winnie nodded. "And what *exactly* did you see?"

Winnie took a swig of the coffee, then she sat quietly for a moment or two. Alexa could see her running the memory of that night through her mind. She took in a deep, careworn breath. "It was a hot one, that night. The air was so thick you could cut it with a knife, but it had better have been pretty sharp. It was about eleven o'clock, I'd say, and me mother wanted to take me upstairs for bed. So she sacked up the last of the kitchen's trash, and I lugged it past the stairs and out the back door of the bar." She lifted her chin toward the door that led from the shop into the sewing room. "Then I dragged it out the back door into the parking lot. There was only one street lamp at that time, and it was hazy out. When I started toward the trash cans, I noticed they were all knocked about. Trash was lying everywhere, and several mangy alley cats were having themselves a feast. I was so upset because I knew I'd be the one scoopin' it all up. It wouldn't be long until me mother would come out and yell, *What in St. Patrick's name is takin' ya so long, Wynona Mulaney?* So, I chased the cats away, and that's when I saw her." She shook her head, slow and pensive. "She was facedown in the middle of the cans. The police said she must've put up quite a fight."

"Tell me about Cora Lee. I know she was a singer, and she worked at Sears. What about her family?"

"Oh, Cora Lee came from money. Her father was a shoemaker right here on Penn Avenue. Baker's Shoes. The shop was on the other end of the Strip. He made the finest and most expensive ladies' shoes around. His wife was a seamstress, much like yourself, only not quite on this scale of things." Winnie waved her hand around the shop. "Mrs. Baker did hems and repairs. I don't think she made clothing. At least, none that me mother could afford, I'll tell ya that."

"I see. Oh, one more thing, were the cans to the right of the door or to the left?" Alexa asked.

"To the right. Why?"

"Garbo sits on top of the chair in my bedroom during the night and looks out over the parking lot. She seems to be keeping some kind of watch, and she's focused on the area below the window and off to the right."

Gasping, Winnie drew her hand to her chest. "Good Lord in the morning. I remember just as I was about to run inside to find me mother, I looked up, and there she was, Garbo was sittin' in that very window, looking down at me."

Hayden Mann was an admirable individual. He looked to be on the shady side of sixty, of average height, thin with just a hint of pudge in his belly. His gray hair was sprinkled with stubborn sprigs of black, refusing to relent to age. He had intelligent, inquisitive, newsman eyes, constantly darting about the room, absorbing every detail.

Hayden's wife, Miffie, was a tiny woman, with a tiny heart-shaped face professionally pulled taut. Perhaps a bit too taut. Her manicured, fiery red fingernails sparkled, as did the huge, diamond cocktail rings on each finger. The woman had not a gray hair upon her bleached-blonde head. She sported a navy blue Nike warm-up suit and slip-on style tennis shoes. "No, I'd prefer we measure or whatever you need to do, out here on the main floor, rather than in one of those little rooms," she'd insisted when Alexa directed Mr. Mann toward the first fitting room. Alexa wasn't quite sure if the woman was uncomfortable with her husband being alone in a room with a strange, younger woman or if she simply wanted to supervise. It really didn't matter. Alexa was quick to comply.

While Alexa took Mr. Mann's measurements, Miffie sat on the sofa chatting on her cell phone while fluffing her stiff hair with those red fingernails. Her Chihuahua, Tinkerbell, who was all decked out in a tutu and pink rhinestone collar, shivered nervously on the ottoman. Garbo had settled herself on the rounded arm of the sofa to glower at Tinkerbell. She made no bones about her distaste for the itty-bitty dog. Every so often, she'd let out a *hiss* and swat at the dog with her claws. Tinkerbell lurched away from the cat, letting out a teeny-weeny *yip*. Obviously, the Chihuahua could see the ghost cat. Miffie was completely baffled over Tinkerbell's rising anxiety.

Pressing the cell phone to her chest, Miffie insisted in her tiny but demanding voice, "Could we hurry this along, *please*? My poor little Tinkie-winkie doesn't like it here at all."

Alexa was more than happy to oblige. By 9:30, she had Mr. Mann measured, fabric for the suit selected, their deposit in the cash drawer, and was waving a cheerful goodbye. Out of the corner of her eye she saw Winnie place the Help Wanted sign in the window.

Her next client, Fiona Quinn, walked through the

door ten minutes early. She was a lovely strawberry blonde with bright green eyes and a stunning figure. She'd brought a gorgeous, beaded, sheath wedding gown with lace three-quarter-length sleeves. The train was plentiful but not outlandishly long. Elegant and tasteful—Alexa's favorite style. The dress didn't need many alterations, a little in the waist and bust area, and several inches of hemming. As Fiona stood on the pedestal with the dress swathed all around her, Garbo slinked through the tiny gap in the door.

Fiona smiled in the mirror. "What a pretty cat."

Almost stabbing herself with a straight pin meant for the hem, Alexa blinked back. "You...you can see that cat?"

In the mirror, Alexa saw Fiona pitch her a quizzical look. "Certainly, can't you? I mean, that is a cat by the door, right?"

"Oh, yes, of course. I...I guess I just didn't realize she was in here."

"She's beautiful. What's her name?"

Alexa was trying to push back her stunned expression. This young woman could actually see Garbo. Up to this moment, only she and Winnie had been able to see the cat. So...why could this woman see her? Finally, she managed, "Garbo."

"You mean, like the old silent film star, Greta Garbo?"

"I believe so, yes."

"What a cool name. I like that." Evidently, Garbo liked the woman. She made herself comfortable at the edge of the pedestal staring up at her. *Weird.* "Oh, she has the most gorgeous blue eyes, doesn't she?"

A little too weird.

As if trying to keep her composure in front of a client who could see the ghost cat wasn't enough, suddenly Bobby Starr was standing near the wine bar. He slipped a bottle from the rack. Alexa couldn't breathe, couldn't swallow. She could feel a hot flush spreading over her cheeks. If Fiona could see the cat, could she see Bobby too? How would she react when she noticed the strange man near the wall to her right? It was time for a little damage control.

"What are you doing here?" she asked the ghost as quietly and pleasantly as she could muster.

Fiona's eyes jerked away from the cat to the mirror, following Alexa's gaze. She searched the reflection, looking for someone in the room. "Who are you talking to?" she inquired.

"I was hoping you'd made up your mind. We're really pressed for time," Bobby said, while examining the bottle's label.

Apparently, Fiona could see the ghost cat but not the ghost. How did that work? Alexa had no idea. Regardless, there was a wine bottle floating in midair. She needed to block Fiona's view of the suspended bottle. More damage control, while making a calm attempt to get rid of the ghost. Looking up at Fiona, she stuck her finger inside her right ear and mouthed the words, "I've got an earbud in." She pointed at Garbo. Thankfully, Fiona's gaze instantly slid toward the cat. "You're right, her eyes are absolutely mesmerizing. I think she likes you, and she's not fond of many people. You must be an animal lover. Cats can always pick out an animal lover. Excuse me for just a moment." Keeping her finger firmly in her ear as if pressing on the faux earbud, she pushed up from her knees to calmly walk toward the wine bar. She positioned her body between Bobby and Fiona, then snatched the bottle from Bobby's hand to whisper, "I've got a client. I can't talk right now. I'll be available in a half hour." She could hear Fiona cooing at the cat in the background.

Bobby pointed at the cat. "Is that...*Garbo*?"

Alexa's tone grew terser by the second. "Yes, it is. Now, *please go.*" Much to her relief, Bobby disappeared. She let out the breath she'd been holding, replaced the bottle, then with a bright smile planted on her lips, she turned back toward Fiona. "I think this dress is absolutely perfect for you, Fiona. When did you say the wedding is?"

"We haven't quite decided, but soon. Actually, we're already married. We got married spontaneously last summer on a cruise ship. This wedding is for the family."

"How fun. Well, I've got all my pins in place. Let me help you get out of that dress so you don't get too many pin-sticks."

Garbo followed Fiona like a lovesick puppy toward the cash desk. She leapt onto the bar to keep a close eye on the lovely strawberry blonde while she paid for the alterations to be made on the dress. Garbo trailed along as Fiona made her way out the front door. Alexa watched through the window to see if the cat would follow her to her Mini-Cooper parked right outside, but Garbo remained inside the shop watching Fiona's departure from the front door. *Thump, thump.* Fiona's poor little Mini-Cooper was the latest victim of the pothole.

Alexa's stomach was churning as she turned away from the window. It was time to tell Bobby Starr she intended to help him find Cora Lee's murderer—if that was actually possible. She grabbed up a cookie from the tray, popped it into her mouth, then noticed a wide-eyed Winnie studying the computer screen at the cash desk. Stealing another cookie, she walked along the bar toward Winnie. "Something wrong?"

"Your next appointment is with Murielle Baker?"

"That's right, one o'clock. Do you know her?"

Winnie swept a white wisp of hair from her eye. "She's Cora Lee's niece. Murielle would've been about fourteen or fifteen when Cora Lee died. She was good friends with me sister, Maggie. She never married. She was a teacher and, like me, favored her independence as opposed to being tied down to one man. She's well into her eighties now, but a strong, capable woman nonetheless."

Just then, Bobby reappeared. "Is the coast clear?"

Alexa's churning stomach now tightened into tiny knots. "Yes, Fiona's gone. So, how does this work, Bobby? How do we investigate a murder that is almost seventy years old?"

"The only way we can: we go back to 1953. But we'll have to be very careful. Pete says we can't do anything to change the future, unless it's a change that comes with an approval, but I'm not sure we'd be aware of that stuff. And we can't do anything to alter reality. Like, trying to prevent Cora Lee's death."

"I don't know. I mean, I've got a business to run. How can I go to 1953 and take care of things here, too?"

"Don't worry, Pete said it will all be taken care of.

I'm not sure what he means, but I trust him. I mean, he's Saint Peter, how can you not trust that?"

Alexa took in a terrified breath. "Anything else?"

"Yeah, we've got to be careful not to run into me. I mean, the me from 1953. Pete said I'll still be there, so I can't run into myself. I'll fill you in on the details of the case when we get there." He held out his hand. "C'mon, we're running out of time."

Alexa looked back at Winnie, whose eyes were wide with fear. "I'll be back...hopefully." Before she could change her mind, she placed her hand in Bobby's. In an instant, her body felt heavy. She squeezed Bobby's hand tightly. She felt like she was being sucked into the floor, a twirling, spinning, uncontrollable vacuum pulling her down, down, down into a deep chasm of darkness. Where was Bobby? Did she still have his hand? She couldn't see anything, except for a spear of light slashing through the void every few seconds. What had she agreed to? Where was she going? More importantly, could she find her way back?

ONE MOMENT ALEXA AND BOBBY were standing hand in hand directly in front of her, and the next they were gone. What was she to do now? How was she supposed to explain to the new clients that the seamstress was not there? Winnie hurried to the bar where she'd seen the bottle of Jameson sitting below it. She snatched up the bottle and, with fumbling fingers, twisted off the lid. She searched under the bar for the shot glasses and, finding none, she lifted the bottle to her lips to take a swig. "I'm startin' to think I might be too old for this job."

Chapter Seven

Beyond

"Are you okay?" Bobby's voice seemed far away. An icy breeze stung Alexa's cheek, bringing her to complete focus. She opened her eyes to find herself standing on the sidewalk along Penn Avenue. She was fairly sure it was Penn. She scanned up the street and down. Yes, it was Penn Avenue, only it didn't look like the street she was familiar with. The thoroughfare wasn't lined with SUVs, or sleek midsize cars of Alexa's time. Rather, the parking spots were filled with cars she'd seen in old movies or the occasional car show Dennis would drag her to on a scorching summer day.

Hunkered deep in the collar of their coats, shoppers scurried along the street. A gentle snow was falling, covering the sidewalk and the parked cars with a powdery skiff. It wasn't July. It couldn't be July, not with snow coming down. The sky was heavy with ashen clouds; it definitely looked like a snow-sky. Pittsburgh's weather could be temperamental, but snow in July? Not hardly.

Just then, she realized she was wearing a hat. She reached up to pull it from her head. Alexa couldn't believe what she was holding—a lovely black cavalier hat adorned with regal coque feathers that curled along the right side. The hat was magnificent. Replacing the hat on her head, she looked down. Wow, she was wearing a black swing coat, stockings, black pumps, and dangling from her elbow was a lovely black leather purse. Amazing style! Quickly, she began to unbutton the coat.

Bobby grabbed her hand. "What are you doing?"

"I've got to see what I'm wearing under this coat."

Bobby glanced up the street and down, then leaned in close. "Can't you wait until we get inside?"

Alexa stilled. "Inside?"

"Yeah..." He nodded toward the building over her shoulder. "*Inside.*"

Turning, Alexa gasped before she could call it back. There it stood in all its heyday and glory, the Lazy Hound Pub. She couldn't believe her eyes. There was no large awning above the storefront; instead, the glass had been painted with an old sleeping hound dog curled up around a mug of beer. A thick foam spilled over the mug while tiny bubbles danced above. In bold green lettering, *The Lazy Hound Pub* corralled the slumbering, floppy-eared, mongrel.

Alexa moved closer to peer through the window. There was the long bar that currently, or rather, in the future, served as her coffee bar and cash desk, only now it was lined with stools. Several patrons sat at the bar, lifting a pint. Tables for four draped with green tablecloths dotted the rest of the open space.

"Are we goin' in or freezin' to death out here?" Bobby asked.

Still dazed and amazed, Alexa flinched. "What month is it?"

"December 1953. I believe it's December 14th. Cora's been gone five months."

Alexa shook her head. "Mom always threatened to kick my butt into next year, but this is going a bit too far."

"Yeah, I guess so. Are you comin'?"

"Yes, of course, let's go in." She hesitated. "Will they recognize you? I mean, you're older, aren't you? Or...do you look the same as you did then?"

Bobby smiled. "So many questions. Guess we'll find out together, won't we?" He made his way to the door and opened it. He appeared surprised when a young girl about seventeen or eighteen with dark blonde hair rushed out of the bar. It seemed she didn't notice Bobby. She glanced over her shoulder, pulled the collar of her coat closer to her throat, then got into a car parked at the curb. *Thump, thump.* The car smacked the pothole as it quickly pulled away.

My God, it's been almost seventy years and PennDOT still hasn't fixed that hole. Time goes by, very little changes. Alexa stepped past Bobby into the warmth of the Lazy Hound. Instantly she took in the pungent smell of beer and stale cigarette smoke lingering on the air. It was 1953. Men and women alike smoked openly in public places. Smoking a cigarette was considered fashionable during this era and not yet deemed dangerous to one's health. Not used to the thick, ashen miasma of secondhand smoke, Alexa coughed.

"Well, if it isn't Detective Bobby Starr," the bartender announced. Through watering eyes, Alexa looked toward the merry Irish accent calling out to Bobby. "You're in early today."

"Guess that..." *Cough, cough.* "Answers my..." *Cough, cough.* "Question," Alexa managed. She covered her mouth, trying to suppress the attack. Tears filled her burning eyes.

"Are you gonna be okay?" There was an undercurrent of concern in Bobby's voice.

"Water..." *Cough, cough.* "I could use a glass of—" Her words fell away, smothered by another round of coughing fits.

"Brian! A glass of water for the lady, please," Bobby hollered across the room. He palmed her elbow to lead her toward the bar. The patrons, a middle-aged man and three young women, turned to stare at her with unease yet befuddled by her plight.

Brian Mulaney. Alexa may have been incapacitated by her lungs, but she recalled reading Brian Mulaney's name in the newspaper—Winnie's father, and the owner of the pub. He wasn't a very big man, about five foot six, a bit stocky with a thick dark-blond head of hair. He rushed to the sink, poured a glass of water from the faucet, then hurried to hand it across the bar to her.

Through the wheezing, she rasped, "Thank you." She took a greedy gulp of the water, hoping it would cure her ill. She felt a doozie of a headache coming on—sinuses.

"Are you gonna be all right, then?" Brian asked. His face was pinched with worry.

Trying to regain her composure, Alexa glanced

askance at the three women sitting at the bar, now huddled close, whispering. Every moment or so, they'd dare a peek at her, then resume their clandestine conversation. The pretty, auburn-haired woman sitting closest tossed Bobby a bewitching smile each time, before returning to the cliquey parlay. The man's interest in Alexa's well-being had waned. He had returned his attention to his beer and the smoldering cigarette in the ashtray before him.

"If ya don't mind my sayin', ya might need something a bit stronger than that water, lass," Brian suggested.

"You might be right," Alexa croaked. "I'll have..." Even though she could feel her sinuses swelling, a great epiphany struck her. So many movies hadn't been released yet, they hadn't even been filmed. So many great lines not yet spoken. What wicked fun.

Brian leaned over the bar. "What did ya say you'll have?"

A sly curl lifted Alexa's lips. "A martini, please. *Shaken,* not stirred."

Brian's brows drew downward, clearly flummoxed by the request. He shrugged his shoulders, then grabbed a martini glass from the mirrored shelves. She checked the reaction of the three women in the mirrors. They too were a bit dumbstruck by the odd petition. Alexa's gaze slid across the mirrors to seek out Bobby's reaction as well. He'd leaned an elbow on the bar, narrowed eyes fixated on Brian gathering the ingredients. Seemed she'd caused quite a stir, and she was enjoying every moment.

"Wait up, chap," the man said in a heavy cockney accent. His face was weathered, maybe from the elements, maybe from the smoking. His eyes were hard. "Let me pay ya for the beer. I need to get back to the shop. Mrs. Baker will be lookin' for me, yeah?" He handed Brian two quarters and a dime, stuck the cigarette between his lips, and slipped from the seat, pulling on an old work jacket while making his way toward the door. He nodded at Bobby, and Bobby returned the subtle greeting.

Brian tossed the change in the cash register, then, snatching up a shaker, he poured gin, then the dry vermouth, then added ice cubes and shook it all around. Finally, Brian poured the mix into the glass, adding an olive. Doubt filling his expression, he lifted the glass high before he handed it to her. "Here's your martini. Stirred *not*, but shaken, and here's to hopin' this drink isn't forsaken."

Everyone chuckled at Brian's impromptu toast. Alexa understood where Winnie got her Irish sense of humor. In the mirrors she could see she had everyone's attention. Boy, at this moment, she was hoping she could trust Ian Fleming and his muse, James Bond.

Acting as if she was accustomed to drinking martinis, and always drank them shaken, Alexa lifted the glass to take a sip. She'd read somewhere that Ian Fleming, the author of the James Bond spy novels, preferred his martinis shaken because he believed stirring the martini diminished the flavor. At this moment she agreed. The cocktail was bursting with zing.

She grinned at Brian. "Perfect."

The auburn-haired woman took a long drag from her cigarette, then blew out the smoke into a tall column. Alexa thought she resembled an imperious dragon.

The woman asked, "So, who is *this*, Bobby?" It wasn't a sociable query. The dragon's tone was probing, sliding dangerously close to a grilling.

"A new client. We need to talk about her case." Grabbing Alexa's hand, he pulled her from the stool. "You can bring your drink along with you."

"Are ya gonna pay for that drink?" Brian asked.

"Put it on my tab."

"You haven't got a tab."

"Start one." With that, he palmed Alexa's elbow, urging her toward the stairs that led to the three apartments above.

As they climbed, Alexa asked, "Who was that woman?"

"Catherine."

"With a C or a K?"

"C—Catherine number two."

Alexa glanced over the railing to meet Catherine's glower. Through the pall of smoke surrounding her, Alexa could see the red-hot flush staining Catherine number two's cheeks. "I don't think she likes me."

"She hates you. Don't feel too bad. She hated Cora too. C'mon, I want to fill you in on the details of this case."

Alexa was about to see her apartment as it was many years ago, when it housed three sets of tenants with one common bathroom. He led her through an open archway into the small, drafty foyer where the bathroom was located directly ahead. The lighting was dim. The walls were painted a dingy white. The stench of stale cigarettes wafted up the staircase. The door to the bathroom was open, but Alexa didn't care to look inside. Just beyond the bathroom door a telephone hung on the wall. It was a black pay phone. The dirty, discolored cord was stretched to its limits, hanging in twisted tangles a good three feet or so below the phone. How amazing was that? Three sets of tenants shared a bathroom and a telephone, and they had to pay for each call individually. Apparently, the apartments didn't have phones. She couldn't begin to imagine. She wondered how much a call would cost. A dime? A quarter? How much time would one be allotted for the call? A minute, or was it an unlimited amount? Again, baffling.

They came upon two doors as they rounded the bend. It was just as Winnie had described. The door farthest to the left and almost against the outside wall was Bobby's. He was sliding the key into the lock.

Alexa tugged at the sleeve of his coat. "How do you know you're not in there?"

"Because it's three o'clock. I'm out somewhere working a case."

Alexa looked to her right. Not far down the hallway was another door. She remembered Winnie saying an older Irish couple lived in that apartment, the Murphys, if her memory served her correctly. She bent forward just a bit to look farther down the deep, dark hallway where the third door stood among the shadows—the Mulaneys' apartment. The largest unit spanned the entire front of the building. She could smell a stew cooking in one of the dwellings. She heard someone laugh and the murmur of conversation from behind the Murphys' door.

"Alexa..." Bobby's voice brought her back to the moment. He was holding the door to his apartment open.

"Let's talk about Cora Lee's death, and what we plan to do."

Just as Alexa was about to step through the doorway, a middle-aged woman wearing a red dress with white polka dots, covered by a full-length, red apron, hastened past. She didn't appear to simply be in a hurry, she seemed flustered, clutching a piece of paper in her right hand. Her quick, heavy footfalls bounded down the staircase as she called out in a frightened voice, "Brian! Brian Mulaney!"

"Who was that?"

"Molly Mulaney."

Still looking after where Molly had just trod, while listening to see if she could hear any conversations, Alexa noted, "She was very upset."

"I find that most women with teenage daughters are *always* upset. That was Elenore or Ellie Mulaney who came out of the pub when we were going in."

"She got into a car that sped off."

"Oh, I didn't notice."

"Maybe that's why you're not a very good detective. Hence, the mess you're, or should I say, *we're* in."

Bobby rolled his eyes. "Brian and Molly's problems with Ellie aren't my concern."

"How do you know? How do you know Ellie's situation doesn't directly or indirectly affect this case?"

"Because, I know."

"You've got *five* unsolved murders, Mr. Starr."

He pitched her a baleful look. "You just want to know what trouble is."

A shrug. "Ma-a-a-y-be."

Letting out a beleaguered sigh, Bobby waved her into

79

his apartment, then closed the door. He lowered his voice. "These walls are paper thin. The old lady next door, Mrs. Murphy, always knows when I've got a woman in here. The next morning, she always gives me—"

Alexa raised a halting hand. "I don't want to know about any of it. Just tell me about Elenore."

He waved his hand at a small table positioned near the window that looked out over the parking lot. "Have a seat."

A dense film of dust and grime covering the window masked the snow falling over the lot. Mothbitten, shabby sheers dangled from a crooked curtain rod. The apartment wasn't small, it was downright miniature. To the right of the door and tucked into a corner was an itty-bitty L-shaped kitchen. Off-white metal cabinets hung above a short, green laminate countertop. Only two cabinets, also metal, a small porcelain sink, and a set of three drawers stood beneath the counter. At the end of the cabinets was a slender stove with a tiny oven. Alexa had never seen such small burners, and there were four of them. The refrigerator was tiny too, a light blue. The fridge would be considered retro in her time, but practical in Bobby's. The floor was a scuffed hardwood that hadn't been swept in quite some time. A layer of dust and some tiny food particles were strewn over the floor. Beyond the fridge was a narrow closet door.

"Hey, now would be a good time to take off that coat," Bobby said.

Alexa unbuttoned the coat and Bobby helped her slip it from her shoulders. She eased the hat from her head, and he set both on the bed. Her dress was stylish and lovely. A black, capped sleeve, full skirt with a delicate sweetheart neckline. And pearls, she was wearing a triple-strand pearl necklace. Good job, Saint Pete!

She crossed the room, past the full-size bed. The sheets were in a tangle, the blanket rumpled near the footboard, and the pillows were crinkled and folded near the headboard. The banged-up nightstand held a dirty, white milk glass hobnail lamp. A clutter of items surrounded the lamp: a red wind-up alarm clock, an overflowing ashtray filled with butts, a smashed cigarette pack, and a small notepad, no pen. She tried to keep a casual demeanor and not stare at the mess as she approached the table. A hotchpotch of paperwork, notebooks, and a scatter of black and white photographs littered the tabletop. Bobby quickly removed a pile of old magazines from one of the two chairs so she could sit. He tossed the magazines onto the bed, then sat down on the chair across the table.

Alexa tried to see how much snow was piling up outside through the grunge on the glass. Her voice was quiet. "You should clean this window. It would let some light in. Make it easier to do paperwork."

"It's fine the way it is," Bobby said in a soft, remorseful voice.

Alexa's gaze slid toward him. She studied his rueful deportment. While Garbo kept a steady guard over the place where her mistress had been left for dead, Bobby preferred a barrier, no matter how thin, between him and Cora Lee's death. Why did he stay? Why didn't he move to a different apartment? A different location altogether? She cleared her throat, hoping to clear the mood. "You were going to tell me about Elenore..."

"Oh, that's right." He lifted an apathetic shoulder. "Same old, same old. Winnie told me her parents don't approve of Ellie's boyfriend. Seems he's not *Catholic*."

"Oh, I see. They'll get it all straightened out, I'm sure."

"Now, are we good?" Bobby asked.

"Mm, one more thing. If you're dead and Cora Lee is dead, why haven't you asked her who killed her?"

"I haven't seen Cora. I'm not sure she's crossed over. I'm hoping after all this is over, we'll..." his voice fell away.

Alexa's heart hurt for him. The silence stretched between them, and she regretted asking the question. "Can you give me some details about Cora Lee's murder? For example, do you know what the murder weapon was? I mean, I know she was strangled, but was she strangled with a cord or by hand? Was the murder weapon found at the scene? Or did they find it at all?"

Cocking his head to one side, Bobby's brows drew down into a deep V. "No wonder Pete wanted you to help out. You sure do know the right questions."

"I watch a lot of CSI programs on..." She searched the room for a television. There wasn't one. "Um, on television. The fact is, you leave something behind wherever you go."

"You mean like a scarf or a glove?"

How was she supposed to go about explaining DNA to someone from the 1950s—long before such technology was considered? Alexa made an attempt. "Not exactly. A scarf or a glove would be a physical object, and yes, that's always a possibility, of course. But what I'm talking about is more...scientific. Like...fingerprints. Only, in my time, we can identify people by blood, hair follicles, skin, and more things than I know."

"Interesting. Hocus pocus." Bobby reached into the pocket of his coat to pull out a pack of cigarettes, Lucky Strikes. He slipped one from the pack, tucked it in his lip, then fished around the pocket until he came up with a lighter.

Alexa whipped up her right hand. "It's not hocus pocus, it's *science*, and I'd *appreciate* if you *don't* smoke. If you recall, it makes me cough."

He tossed her a look that was just this side of a scowl, then chucked the lighter atop the mess on the table, leaving the cigarette to dangle between his lips. Hooking his right elbow over the back of the chair, he explained, "They weren't sure what was used to strangle her. Although, they eliminated a rope because there were no rope burns on her neck. The coroner suggested it could have been a strap of some kind. Maybe leather, something handy, like a belt. And no, the weapon was not found at the scene or anywhere else."

Alexa's thoughts were ripping through her mind and questions came out just as fast. "Was there anyone who didn't like Cora Lee? Was there an ex-husband, fiancé, or boyfriend in the picture? Or do you think she was simply a random victim? A lone woman in a dark parking lot, late at night. Easy prey."

"Everyone loved Cora. I don't think anyone had it in for her. She had no ex-anything. I was her first. Her first for...everything." Another somber shrug. "The police never came up with any suspects."

Alexa's eyes perused the pathetic apartment. Good going, Cora, she thought, then immediately felt bad about the muse. Not everyone lived like she and Dennis had. Evidently, Cora Lee married for love, which is, and always had been, a noble gesture. Some women lived to regret it, and some flourished within that decision. On the other hand, she had to wonder how Cora Lee's parents felt about the match. Winnie claimed the Bakers were wealthy entrepreneurs. Most hard-working, self-made couples didn't approve of their daughters marrying into poverty.

Shoving her thoughts aside, Alexa inquired, "Were there any persons of interest?"

Again, he looked at her with a stymied expression. "Isn't that the same thing?"

"I...I'm not sure."

"Well, it *sounds* like the same thing. What kind of shows do you watch again?"

"Never mind. Was Cora Lee the only strangulation victim in or around the Pittsburgh area in the past year or so?"

Bobby rubbed the nape of his neck. His voice sounded hopeless, almost defeated. "I dunno." Then, his eyes widened. "Wait a minute." He straightened in his seat. "I remember hearing Clifton talking about a girl being murdered near the Stanley Theater, over there on Seventh Street. And I'm pretty sure I heard him say she was strangled."

The Stanley Theater was long gone in Alexa's time. In the late 1980s, the once-popular music hall had been refurbished, replaced, and renamed the Benedum Center, currently home to the Pittsburgh Ballet and Pittsburgh Opera. She knew exactly what theater Bobby was talking about.

"When was she murdered? Before or after Cora Lee? Clifton *who*?"

"You sure do come up with questions fast, lady." Bobby's eyes searched the floor as if he could see this Clifton person discussing the murder. Finally, his eyes lifted to meet hers. "His name is Clifton Slater. He's a big-shot police detective for the city. He was tellin' another cop about it downstairs in the pub about two months before my Cora was killed." His voice lifted. Hope had returned. "Yeah, that's right. It was just a day or two before the big Memorial Day parade. I remember, because the cop had just finished his mounted police training, and the parade was going to be his first assignment. He was nervous as he—I mean, he was *really* nervous." He reached for the lighter. Alexa raised a brow in warning. Thinking better of it, he pulled his hand back.

"*Now* we're getting somewhere. Did he, by chance, mention the girl's name?"

"I don't think so."

"No worries. We can look it up. Where's your lap—" Alexa swallowed back her words. There was no laptop. There was no cell phone. Heck, there wasn't even a land-line phone in the man's apartment—only a pay phone in the hall. What good was that?

"My...*what*?"

"Never mind. I wasn't thinking. Wait...did you say *Clifton Slater*?"

"I did. Do you know him?"

"I might know his relatives." She waved her hand. "That's not important. We need to find out the girl's name and get some information on her *and* her death."

85

"Why?"

"Because her death may be connected to your wife's." She pushed up from the chair and gathered her coat and hat from the bed. "Let's go to the library."

"Why are we going to the library?"

"To look for newspaper articles about a girl strangled near the Stanley a day or two before Memorial Day, and hopefully her obituary." She slipped her arms into the sleeves of the coat, hiking it up onto her shoulders. "Unless, you would care to ask Clifton Slater about her. It would save us a ton of time."

"Not a chance. Let's just say, we're not exactly close. He hates private detectives, and I'm not fond of the police."

Finding a cracked, dirty mirror mounted on the wall, Alexa fixed the feathers on the hat to curl around her chin, then smiled. "The library it is."

They made their way down the stairs slowly. Alexa wasn't sure if Bobby was watching out for Catherine, or for himself—Bobby Starr from 1953. When they reached the halfway point, they noticed the pub was starting to come alive. Several tables were occupied, and a din of conversation and laughter filled the room. Catherine and her friends were still sitting at the bar. Molly and Brian Mulaney were talking with a tall, handsome man sporting a long, black overcoat and a fedora. Grabbing Alexa's arm, Bobby pulled up short.

"What's wrong?"

"*That* is *Detective* Clifton Slater."

Alexa felt her pulse hitch. Detective Clifton Slater was the spitting image of his...grandson, Cliff? Rather,

Cliff was the spitting image of his grandfather, Clifton. It didn't matter. This man standing in the pub reminded her of the man she couldn't stop thinking about in her own time. She had grown up next door to Cliff, but she was fairly sure his father was not a police detective. She was certain Mr. Slater operated his own accounting firm downtown. It appeared Cliff followed in his grandfather's footsteps. Perhaps accounting wasn't exciting enough for Cliff.

She shook her arm free of Bobby's grip to hurry down a few steps. Bobby rushed after her. "Where are you going?" he demanded.

"To ask Detective Slater about the girl. You remember, the girl who was strangled near the Stanley Theater."

"Of course I remember. You can't just march over there and ask him about that."

"Watch me." She attempted to move forward. Bobby tugged her back.

"He's talking with Brian and Molly. She looks upset. Something's up."

Alexa hesitated. Molly Mulaney was in tears. She shook the paper in her hand at the detective. She had a feeling the problem had everything to do with Elenore. She sympathized. However, if they were going to solve Cora Lee's murder in the next three days, they needed information, and they needed it *now*. "You're right. This gives *you* a chance to find out what's going on with the Mulaneys, and *me* an opportunity to engage in a conversation with Detective Slater about the girl."

"*What*?"

"Oh, for heaven's sake, follow my lead." Without

giving Bobby another chance to object, Alexa took him by the hand, scurried down the stairs straight toward the Mulaneys and Detective Slater. Alexa paused. There, on the last stool near the staircase, sat a little girl no more than eight years of age, Winnie. She looked adorable, wearing a red and white pleated, plaid suspender dress and a darling little white blouse. Her hair wasn't snowy white, but rather, a golden blonde. A book was propped open before her. She wrote with great concentration on a sheet of yellow lined paper.

Turning her attention to Winnie's rattled parents, Alexa urged Bobby with her eyes. He awkwardly blurted out, "What's wrong?"

The Mulaneys and Detective Slater turned. Molly's eyes were watery and swollen, her nose and cheeks red and puffy. "Oh, Mr. Starr, it's Ellie. She's run away with that boy." She gave Bobby the paper. "She left this letter saying she loved him and they were going off to get married. We've got to find her before she makes a *terrible* mistake." She leaned in close to whisper, "He's *Jewish*, you know."

Bobby's gaze slid to Alexa, who noticed Winnie turn her attention toward her mother, roll her eyes, then return to her homework. Detective Slater tried to calm Molly. "Mrs. Mulaney, your daughter is of age to make this decision. Unless Mr. Finkler forced her to leave against her will, I'm afraid there's nothing I, or the police department, can do about this." His voice softened. "I'm sorry, Molly."

Molly turned to her husband. "Brian, you've got to do something."

Brian enveloped her in his arms. "I'm afraid there's not much we can do. We've lost a daughter. She's not welcome here anymore. Not if she marries that boy." Clearly broken-hearted, Molly dropped her face into his chest and wept.

Alexa blinked back. "Wait...what?"

Quickly, Bobby took her by the elbow. "It's a family matter, Alexa. We shouldn't get involved."

"But...they shouldn't—"

Bobby leaned in close. "It's *1953*, Alexa. Things were much different than they are in your day. Leave it be. Remember, Pete said it's not our place to change these events. I thought you wanted to talk with Slater."

"I do, but—"

"Well, there he goes. You'd better hurry if you want to catch him," Bobby said, as he jerked his head toward the door.

She hadn't noticed the detective step away. Clifton Slater was almost out the door. Alexa trotted toward him. "Detective Slater..." When he turned, her breath caught. He had the same disarming eyes as Cliff, and when she got back to her time, she needed to make things right so she could look into those eyes again.

"Can I help you, miss?"

"I...I..." She hadn't thought this moment through. She needed to come up with something good within the next five seconds. "You know, it's a shame that...that the Mulaneys are shunning their daughter—"

"Not my business, miss." He placed his hand on the door to push it open.

Alexa stepped forward. "I know, but...I have no doubt

those poor parents of that girl who was murdered behind the Stanley last May would love to have their daughter back."

His hand dropped away from the door. He turned to meet her gaze. "Do you know something about Louise Kinsley's death?"

Alexa threw her hands in the air. "That's her name, *Louise*. No, but I remember hearing about it, and I feel badly that this family has a living daughter and Louise's family…"

"Look, it isn't my job to reconcile families. The Mulaneys are devout Catholics. I wouldn't be surprised if the Finklers feel the same way about their son. As for the Kinsleys, if you know something about Louise's death, anything at all, you'd be helping that family heal. Miss…"

"Owl, Alexa Owl. I'm sorry, I don't know anything about it, but if I did, I wouldn't hesitate to tell you what I know."

"Nice to meet you, Miss Owl. I have a bit of solid advice for you—get away from Bobby Starr. He's bad news." With that, he pressed through the door into the cold and bluster.

Alexa turned away from the door to see Bobby leaned in close, talking with Catherine. The conversation appeared rather chummy. Okay, well, she would be his third wife, the second Catherine. The Mulaneys were gone, as was Winnie. She figured Molly herded the little girl upstairs and Brian felt his wife could use some comforting. They were making a terrible decision about Elenore, but Bobby was right, it was not their place to change these or any other events.

Without warning, her body felt heavy. She felt that same pull, the same vacuum as if she were being sucked through the floor when she and Bobby traveled to 1953. Wait...where was she going? Bobby wasn't with her! Surely, she wasn't being drawn into a different dimension, a different time lapse—not alone! No! Wait! She hadn't gathered all the information she required to solve Cora Lee's...

Chapter Eight

Flash in the Pan

Alexa's head was throbbing. She pressed her fingers against both temples, eyes squeezed closed, when she felt a gentle caress on her shoulder. "It's been a long day, lass. Are ya feelin' all right?" Winnie's sweet Irish voice was as gentle as the caress.

Hold up...*Winnie*? How did...Alexa opened her eyes to find her white-haired, Irish friend standing in front of her, concern filling her gaze. Dazed and confused, then a sudden burst of alarm coiling through her, Alexa grabbed her hand. "Winnie...how long have I been gone? How did you explain my absence to the customers?"

Winnie patted her hand. "Calm down, now. You disappeared, then thankfully, you reappeared just a few seconds later, no worse for the wear. Although, if you don't mind my sayin', you were a bit...stiff. It was almost like part of you was missing, the part that was your personality, I'm sorry to say. You don't remember any of it, then?" Alexa didn't have to think, she shook her head no. "Hm, you must be living in a split-time situation or some kind of time warp. Oh! If only Rod Serling could see us now!"

Alexa chuckled. "I know, right?"

"By the way, you hired that young girl over there as your salesgirl." She nodded toward a young girl leaning her elbow on the bar, resting her cheek in her palm, her head bobbing as if she were about to doze off at any given second. At a quick guess, she looked to be twenty, maybe twenty-one. She was about five foot three, slim; her chin-length hair was a light brunette with dark purple streaks throughout. She wore a short, navy blue, polka-dotted dress and a sage green cardigan sweater, the sleeves pushed up to her elbows. Chic style.

Alexa's brows furrowed. "Really? What's her name?"

"Stacia." Winnie said. She picked up the bottle of Baileys Irish cream from the bar and poured a bit into her coffee mug.

"How's she doing so far?"

"She's only been on the job for two hours. But she's spilled the coffee twice, the first was in a customer's lap." She took a gulp from the mug.

"Aren't you going to put some coffee in with that Baileys?" Winnie shook her head no. "Okay. So, was the client upset?

"Murielle was wet, but fine." Winnie lifted the mug. "Here's to hopin' the lass does better tomorrow."

"*Murielle Baker*? Cora Lee's niece?"

"That's right. But you handled it fine. She walked out of here with a smile on her face and a nip in her step."

Alexa rolled her eyes. "Ugh, did I have the presence

of mind to ask her any questions about Cora Lee? And if I did, do you remember what she said?"

"No, you didn't mention Cora Lee at all. But you went about your business without a hitch. Why, you set straight to working on Mr. Mann's suit jacket, got it all laid out, and the fabric cut. Very diligent in your work."

A *crash*, a *splash*, and a *thud* made Alexa and Winnie's attention flash toward Stacia, who was holding her hand up. "Oh! I'm sorry! I'll clean it up! I just need some paper towels." She rushed through the door where the office and the small kitchen were located. A cup of what looked like pop had fallen from the bar, spilling over the floor. Alexa was thankful the cup was made of plastic and not glass. Needless to say, Stacia was fully awake now.

Shaking her head, Winnie put in, "My stars, she's as clumsy as a drunken leprechaun. Oh, by the way, your sister called. You were busy with Murielle so Stacia took a message."

"What did she want?"

Winnie made her way along the bar toward the cash desk. Her nose crinkled as she picked up a sopping wet piece of paper, ink bleeding down the page. She held it in the air by her fingertips. "Only the good Lord knows."

Alexa sighed.

EXHAUSTED DIDN'T BEGIN TO DESCRIBE Alexa after she'd taken a long, hot, shower, slipped into a comfortable nightgown, and climbed into her bed. Moonlight spilled through the window, illuminating a watchful Garbo. As she perked her ears, the cat's tail dangled over the back of the chair, slowly sweeping back and forth over the tufted fabric. What did Garbo see this night? A rat dashing across the parking lot to the garbage cans? Someone walking along 25th Street? Or apparitions of a murder from long ago? Alexa didn't care to think about that.

She propped several pillows behind her back and settled her laptop on her knees, her small notepad and a pen on the pillow next to her. It was time to glean what information she could about Louise Kinsley. The blue hue from the laptop's screen cast a soft glow around her. What was the name of that site again? Find a Death. Yep, that was it. Finding the site, she typed *Louise Kinsley murder, May 1953.*

Alexa was amazed at how little information there was on such subjects. Perhaps the news media of the past didn't dwell on murder investigations as they do nowadays. Of course, the information hadn't been logged into too many databases because of how old the information was. It was considered irrelevant, she supposed, but not to her, not at this moment. Luckily, the site had two articles listed, and Miss Kinsley's obituary. Hm, someone, somewhere didn't consider this information irrelevant. She clicked on the obit first...

Louise Marie Kinsley passed away suddenly on Thursday, May 28th, 1953. She was born August 5, 1928, in Pittsburgh, Pennsylvania. Daughter of Sarah Kinsley and the late Thomas Kinsley. She was an usher at the Stanley Theater for six years. She is survived by her mother, Sarah Kinsley, brother Thomas, and two sisters, Clara Barnes and Melva Kinsley. The Kinsley family will receive visitors at their home, Cresson Street, Wilkinsburg, starting at 11 A.M. on Monday, May 30th. Interment will be at Allegheny Cemetery, Butler Street.

Interesting. Cora Lee was murdered behind the pub after her singing gig, and Louise was murdered behind the theater after she finished her evening as an usher. Was that the only link between the two women? Cora Lee came from a family with the financial means to provide visitation hours at a funeral home. Evidently, Louise's family could not afford such a luxury. Her viewing took place in the family's residence. Alexa took up the notepad and pen, then flipped past the information she'd scribbled down about Cora Lee's family to a fresh page. Quickly, she jotted down the names of Louise Kinsley's family members and her mother's address. Perhaps she and Bobby should visit Mrs. Kinsley to see what extra-curricular activities, if any, Louise participated in. Bobby wasn't sure if Detective Slater said Louise was strangled. She clicked on the first newspaper article published in the *Pittsburgh Daily Times...*

Usher Found Dead Behind Stanley Theater

The police were called to the Stanley Theater in the wee hours of May 28th when the body of Louise Kinsley was found behind the theater. Miss Kinsley had been an usher for the Stanley Theater for six years. Fellow usher and friend of Kinsley, Marion Hill, stated that the performance by Peggy Lee had filled the theater to capacity the evening before. Hall said that Miss Kinsley decided to go out the back door of the theater to avoid the lingering crowds, hoping to get an autograph from Miss Lee.

Miss Kinsley's body was discovered by a vagrant, who was questioned and released. The coroner revealed Miss Kinsley had been strangled. An investigation is ongoing at this time. ~ Ray Howell/Pittsburgh Daily Times

Alexa wrote down Marion Hill's name two spaces below the list of Kinsley family names. If Marion was a friend of Louise's, as the article indicated, she may know intimate details of Louise's life. It was something worth considering. She paused, letting out a burdened and weary breath, and at that moment, Garbo padded across the laptop's keyboard. She looked up at Alexa with those spellbinding blue eyes. She purred while smoothing her white body against the screen. The blue hue transformed her white, transparent image into a blue, furry feline. Then the cat hopped away from the laptop to curl up on the pillow next to Alexa. Still purring, Garbo faced the window, now keeping her heedful watch at a distance.

How strange. Garbo had not once approached her, let alone come into her bed. Alexa studied the screen filled with limited information on Louise's murder, and she had to wonder if Garbo was trying to tell her something. Something like...you're heading in the right direction, Owl.

Her phone dinged, calling her attention to a text message. She picked the phone up from the nightstand and the screen announced a message from...*Cliff Slater*! Alexa's heart skipped a beat. What was this effect Cliff had on her? She clicked on the text that simply read, *hi there.*

Suddenly, she was wide awake and sitting straight up. She thumbed: *Hi.*

A moment later, Cliff replied: *Got time for coffee tomorrow?*

Garbo twisted her head to gaze up at her. Alexa recognized a sense of reproach in the cat's eyes. "Yeah, I know, pretty kitty. This whole Bobby Starr, guardian angel, Cora Lee murder thing couldn't have come at a worse time. C'mon, this could possibly be a serious romance we're talking about here." In one swift move, Garbo bounded from the pillow onto the chair, up onto the back, then, wrapping her tail around her body, she looked out onto the moonlit parking lot. Alexa plopped back against the pillow. Her heart sank. Letting out a beleaguered sigh, she opened a new tab on her laptop to check her schedule for tomorrow. Her first appointment was at one o'clock, a bride and her four bridesmaids. She thumbed: *How about morning coffee? Nine?*

Within a few seconds, he responded: *Nine works. Zeke's Coffee—it's right there on Penn, not too far from your shop.*

She replied: *I'll be there!*

Immediately, she texted Winnie asking if she could arrive at the shop around 8:30 tomorrow morning.

It was just after nine o'clock when Alexa pressed through the door at Zeke's Coffee. She found the shop and the customer seated at the counter in the window very charming. Cliff greeted her with that oh, so handsome smile, and it occurred to her how much his smile matched his grandfather's. "Good morning, Detective Slater. I see you're drinking your coffee black. Must be a habit," she said.

He lifted his mug. "Of course, it's the original black magic. I took the liberty of ordering you a coffee and brought some creamer and sugars over. Hope that's okay."

"It's perfect. And an assortment of Danishes too." She slipped into the chair next to him, hooking her purse over the back.

He pitched her an ornery grin. "Diabetes on a plate to get your day going." She laughed. His grin widened. "How did your first day at the shop go?"

"It was very...interesting. I've got a full afternoon, a bridal party. This morning was pretty open, so I'm glad you could make an early coffee. I was wondering, what made you decide to become a detective? Wasn't your father an accountant?" She opened the small cup of creamer and poured it into her coffee.

"Yep. He had an accounting firm downtown. Not what I wanted to do, sit in a cubicle all day poking at a calculator. No thanks. I took after my grandfather. He was a police detective back in the day."

"Nice. Was your dad upset that you didn't take over his firm?"

"Not at all. He understood. My brother runs the firm now. Dad's retired, or should I say, semi-retired. He goes into the office about twice a week to make sure Sean's doing a good job. It's probably a good thing, gets him outta Mom's hair for a couple hours. So, you and your sister are selling the house, then?"

Alexa's hand slapped her forehead as she winced. "Oh! That's right. Natalyn called yesterday afternoon and I never called her back. She probably thinks I've lost my mind. You probably do too after the other day."

Cliff held up his hand. "No worries. I figured you were just under a ton of stress. Hey...I was wondering, would you like to have dinner Saturday night? Maybe a movie?"

Second chances. That's what this was, a second chance at romance, and a second chance with Cliff Slater. Alexa's heart swelled. Better yet, by Saturday this whole Bobby Starr thing should be laid to rest once and for all. Surely Saint Peter didn't expect her to assist Bobby Starr in all three murder cases he needed to make right. Surely he intended for her to help in this one and only case. Surely he had someone else in mind for the other two cases Bobby was required to solve. Surely. Smiling, she had no doubt there was a gleam in her eye when she replied, "I'd love that." She took a sip of her coffee. Man, it tasted sooo good.

THE MORNING COFFEE DATE was short-lived. Cliff had to get moving on his cases. So, with a Saturday time set for their real date, each got into their separate vehicles and went their separate ways...until Saturday.

Sipping on a refill of her coffee, Alexa had driven down Penn Avenue one block and was sitting at a red light when that feeling started. That vacuum pulling her down, down, down into a different dimension, a different century. She could feel her heart starting to race. She was at a stop light, for crying out loud! Would her Lexus move forward when the light turned green? Would she still be in the car, even if she, the real she, was tunneling out of control toward 1953? Winnie said she was present at the shop while she was actually gone, and she was hoping this time would be the same!

"I used to go to the same church as Shirley Jones when I lived in Charleroi. I can sing every bit as good as she can. I'm as pretty as she is too. I'll bet I can win that Miss Pittsburgh contest next year. I've got to have my application in by February first…"

A young woman's voice made Alexa's eyes open. She had left her Lexus behind at the intersection and was currently sitting in the Lazy Hound Pub, two stools down from Catherine and her friends. She had to wonder how much time Catherine and her pals spent belly up to the bar.

"I dunno, Mitzi, her daddy owns Jones Brewing. I'll bet that had a lot to do with her winning that contest. Your dad works in the steel mill. Her daddy makes Stoney's Beer. Your daddy makes steel. It's hardly the same," Catherine pointed out.

Alexa shook her head to push out the cobwebs. She turned to her right to find Catherine puffing on a cigarette. She was wearing an emerald green, full-skirt shirt dress. The lapels and pockets were accented in white piping. Mitzi's face bunched in disappointment. Evidently, Catherine's opinion carried a lot of weight. Mitzi tossed the newspaper she was holding onto the bar.

"Someone said she's getting a big interview with the *Pittsburgh Daily Times*," Catherine's other friend, who was sitting on the other side of Mitzi, supplied. "Is that true?"

Catherine blew a dragon's breath of smoke into the air. Her lips curled. "Now, how would I know about that, Sandy?"

Alexa felt bad for Mitzi. Seemed neither of her good friends were very supportive. Alexa stood and a flash of gold caught her eyes. Oh my, she was wearing the loveliest gold, A-line, semi-swing skirt dress with a playful Peter Pan collar. A line of five gold buttons marched down the right side of the bodice from the collar. Saint Peter was very in tune with her tastes, even when it came to an era she did not belong in. She supposed he was trying to make her feel as comfortable as possible in an uncomfortable situation, a situation she did not want any part of. On her lap she found the black leather purse. Not what she would've chosen with this dress. Still, whatta guy!

"I think you're a very pretty girl, Mitzi. And if you sing as well as you say, you should definitely try to win that contest. I mean, hey, why not?" Alexa stirred the pot.

Catherine spun on her stool to face Alexa. "Oh, I didn't see you there. Where's Bobby?"

Alexa glanced about the bar. He was not present. "I haven't the foggiest idea." Grabbing up her purse, she slipped from the stool to make her way toward the door.

Catherine quickly followed. "I'm sure you don't. Here's a little tip for you: don't get too comfortable, honey. Cuz you're just a flash in the pan for Bobby. He'll move on in a day or so. If he hasn't already."

"Whew! That's a relief." Turning, she leaned in close

to whisper, "I'm just using him for sex." Gasping, Catherine's eyes popped so wide Alexa feared she would have to catch her eyeballs in her hands. With Bobby's future third wife completely engulfed in shock, Alexa whirled to walk out the door.

"You're nothing but a *tramp*! Just like that *Cora Lee*!" Catherine bit out.

Alexa came to an immediate halt. She spun on her heels and marched directly back to Catherine number two. "What does *that* mean?"

"Tramp: floozy, trollop, hussy, wh—"

Alexa whipped her hand up. "I'm perfectly aware what a *tramp* is, *girlfriend*. I want to know why you would call *Cora Lee* such a thing."

Catherine's mouth dropped open. She attempted to speak but nothing came out. Alexa couldn't decide if she was taken aback by the fact that she wasn't trying to defend herself or if dragon-lady was stunned by her question. Reconciled with her voice, Catherine stepped in close. "I have it on good authority that Cora Lee was not wearing her wedding ring when they found her body." She glanced furtively about the bar, then added, "You know what *that* means. Cora Lee was stepping out on Bobby."

She attempted to turn away. Alexa caught her by the arm. "You said you had this information on *good authority*. Who told you about the ring?"

"That's none of your business," Catherine snapped.

"None of my business or are you making it up as you go along? It's easy to accuse someone who can't defend themselves of infidelity, isn't it?" Tapping her fingertips on her lips, she made a big show of deep consideration. "Hm, it's quite possible that Bobby could find out on *good authority* that you're spreading nasty rumors about his late wife, as in his *murdered* wife."

"You wouldn't—"

"*Try me.* C'mon, put your money where your mouth is. *Who* told you?"

Catherine's lips pressed into a hard, tight line. Her fists tightened into balls at her sides. Again, she surveyed the bar. Even her girlfriends had returned to their drinks and cigarettes. Tersely, she whispered, "I've had a few dates with Ray Howell." She jabbed Alexa in the chest, hard. "But you didn't hear it from me. And if it gets back that you did use my name, you'll be meeting Cora Lee sooner than you planned." She spun around and flounced back to her stool at the bar between Mitzi and Sandy.

Ray Howell...Ray Howell...where did she know that name from?

"We gotta get outta here," Bobby said, grabbing her by the shoulders from behind.

She managed not to jump two feet in the air. Rather, she asked, "Who's Ray Howell?"

He snatched her coat from the rack inside the door. "Reporter from the *Pittsburgh Daily Times.* C'mon, let's go. I'm coming down the sidewalk."

"You're *what*?"

"The me from 1953 is comin' to the Hound for a beer. We gotta go out the back *now*!" Taking Alexa by the hand, they trotted toward the door at the farthest reach of the bar. Askance, Alexa saw Bobby wave to Catherine as he held the door open for Molly, who was carrying a big box of pretzels. As the door was slamming closed, she caught a quick glimpse of Catherine's glare. No doubt she was agitated by his hasty retreat with the current flash in the pan.

"Hey, Catherine, buy ya a beer?"

Catherine spun on her stool to find Bobby standing directly beside her. Her gaze flashed to the back door, then cut toward him. She stammered, "Bobby...how did you get back so fast?"

BOBBY SLID TO A STOP in the parking lot behind the Hound. "I was hopin' Pete would send you back soon. We're runnin' outta time—"

"What were you doing while I was gone?"

He held her coat up for her to slip into it. "Does it matter?"

Pushing her arms through the sleeves of the coat, Alexa rolled her eyes. "God, I hope not. In any case, there're two people I want to talk to *immediately*. A woman named Sarah Kinsley, and that reporter for the *Times*, Ray Howell. Oh, and possibly a woman named Marion Hill."

"Other than Howell, I don't know those people. Were they friends of Cora's?"

"No. Sarah Kinsley is the mother of another murdered woman, Louise Kinsley. She was the woman who was strangled behind the Stanley Theater. Marion Hill was a good friend of Louise's. Friends tend to know more about a girl's personal affairs than a mom does. Ray Howell reported on both murders, Louise's and Cora Lee's." She hesitated. The next part would be touchy, and she had to tread easy. "Um...by the way, I also found out that Cora Lee was not wearing her wedding band when they found her body."

"I know. But that doesn't mean—"

"No. It doesn't, Bobby, but we need to see if there's a connection between Louise's death and Cora Lee's. The only way we can do that is by talking to these people. Sarah lives in Wilkinsburg. How are we going to get there?"

There it was again, Bobby's boyish smirk, and she couldn't decide if, at this moment, it was a good sign or a really bad one. He said, "C'mon. My car's parked just a few spots down from the Hound."

"But I thought you said you just walked into the bar for a beer."

"I did, and I am. Which means Catherine will keep me busy for a couple hours, and I *always* leave the keys under the front mat. Let's go."

They hurried along 25th Street until they reached the corner of Penn Avenue. Bobby stopped to survey the front of the Lazy Hound. Alexa knew what he was considering: they needed to pass by the large front window undetected. After all, his counterpart was now sitting at the bar with Catherine and her friends. The last thing they needed was for someone to notice another Bobby Starr strolling past the window, and the window was way too low for them to simply duck—they'd have to crawl on their knees to get by unseen. *Not happening—not in this dress!*

"Let's cross the street, go up the other side, then cross back," Alexa suggested.

"Good idea."

They crossed Penn Avenue. Staying hunkered close to the store fronts on the other side, they crossed back over the street almost a block away. "Hold up," Bobby said when they arrived at an old, flat, beige-colored, rusty, dented, 1940-something Chevy. Alexa shivered on the sidewalk, watching him yank several times before the driver's side door reluctantly creaked open. She thought the door was going to fall off the vehicle and onto the street. He dug around on the floor until he victoriously held up a pair of keys. "Just where I always leave them."

"This is your car?"

"It's not pretty, but it gets me where I'm going...most of the time."

Having no choice but to accept this as an *it is what it is* moment, she pulled the passenger door open and slid into the car. "Well, let's hope this is one of those times, Starr."

Bobby got in the car, slammed the door closed, it bounced open, slammed the door closed, it bounced open, then slammed it harder and it clicked. He twisted the key in the ignition. The Chevy choked and coughed and stalled. He shot a withered smile at Alexa and tried again. The old clunker resisted several more times but finally turned over, grunting to a jittering start. He shoved the gear-shift around, more grinding, more complaining, then at last, the car jolted forward. "See, I told you it runs."

"Impressive."

Chapter Nine

Handy Information

"Can I help you?" The woman who spoke through the screen door looked drawn and emaciated. Her green and white plaid housedress drooped on her boney frame. Her blue eyes were sunken and her mouth was drawn downward in what appeared to be a perpetual frown.

"Good afternoon, Mrs. Kinsley. My name is Alexa Owl. I wondered if I could talk to you about your daughter, Louise?"

Her voice was soft and watery. "Louise? What do want to know? Are you with the insurance company or that nice man from the *Times*?"

"No, ma'am. We're...um...Detective Starr and I are investigating two murders in the Pittsburgh area, and we were hoping you might shed some light on the...the... um, investigation."

"Two? What other murders are you investigating?"

"Cora Lee Starr. She was—"

"Oh, yes, I remember. She was strangled just like my

Louise. Only she was killed somewhere in the Strip." Her sad eyes slid toward Bobby. "You're Detective Starr? If I remember the article in the paper, it said her husband was a detective. Is that you?"

"Yes, ma'am. Cora was my wife. Do you mind if we come in?"

Mrs. Kinsley glanced over her shoulder. Alexa recognized that look. She was trying to determine if her house was clean enough for company. She could see the woman contemplating the state of her household versus finding Louise's killer. Justice for her daughter won out. "Yes, please, come in." She unlocked the screen door and held it open for them.

The house was an old-style Pittsburgh three-story home. A staircase was to the left, a man's short, winter coat flung over the newel at the base of the stairs. The living room to the right, and a hallway that led to a small kitchen directly ahead. Most likely, there was a formal dining room off the kitchen. Mrs. Kinsley closed and locked the screen door, then did the same with the front door. It was obvious her daughter's murder had shaken her faith in the human race. Alexa couldn't blame her a bit.

Her pink slippers made a scratching sound as she shuffled across the wooden floor toward the living room. "I'm so sorry for your loss, Detective Starr. Losing a loved one is bad enough, but to lose them to something as heinous as a murder is beyond words." She directed them to a couch along the far wall. The room was plain, but well kept, as was the rest of the house that they could see. She eased into a rocking chair near the picture window. She pulled a dainty lace handkerchief from the pocket of her dress and, with shaking hands, she wiped her eyes. "Now, how can I help you?"

"Some of the questions I ask may be the same ones the police have asked, but our investigation is separate, on a more personal level."

"I understand. Go on..."

"Excuse me." A man's voice broke through the conversation. They turned to see a tall, well-muscled man wearing a pair of old jeans held up by suspenders over a dingy T-shirt. His sandy hair was on the longer side, shaggy, and rather...winsome. He held a wooden toolbox in his left hand. "I've fixed that leak in the kitchen, Mrs. Kinsley. Is there anything else that needs looked after?"

"No, not today, John. Thanks so much. Just leave your bill on the kitchen table, and I'll take care of it tomorrow. If that's okay?"

John's gaze landed on Alexa. He studied her for several moments, his eyes slid to Bobby, and then back to Mrs. Kinsley. "Good enough. I'll stop by tomorrow. You have a nice day now."

"Thank you, John." The man nodded at Bobby and Alexa, then grabbed up his coat hanging on the newel and made his way out the front door. "That was John Hermann. He's a handyman. All the widows in the area use him. He's dependable, does a good job, and he's *affordable*. It's good to have someone you can count on. He's married." Leaning forward, she lowered her voice. "I was always wishing he was single. Maybe he and my Louise—oh, but it wasn't meant to be, I suppose." She sagged back into the rocker. She reminded Alexa of an old, used-up rag doll.

Through the window, Alexa watched the captivating handyman step off the porch and saunter down the sidewalk. "Yes, he seems very nice. Mrs. Kinsley, was Louise dating anyone before her death?"

"I don't think so. Louise was a quiet girl. Kept to herself. She loved to read. Her favorite was Jane Austen." She managed a smile. "Not that she didn't have friends, she certainly did, but she never mentioned a man or anyone special."

"Do you know who her closest friend was?" Bobby asked.

"Marion, Marion Hill. They've been friends since high school. They worked at the theater together. She lives in her parents' house. They're both gone now." She pointed. "It's right up the street, four doors, straight up Cresson Street."

"Do you think she'd mind if we stopped by to talk with her?" Alexa inquired.

"I don't think so. She's been so upset over Louise's... death. She stops by almost every day to check in on me. She always brings me something she's baked. She's such a sweet girl."

"Thank you, Mrs. Kinsley. I think we'll take a walk up to her house now," Alexa said. She stood and Bobby followed suit.

Mrs. Kinsley pushed up from the rocker and led them toward the foyer. "I'll give Marion a call to let her know you're coming, that is, if no one's on the line. I'm on a party line, you know. That Agnes Welton down the street monopolizes the phone lines something awful."

"A *what* line?" Alexa asked.

Bobby leaned in. "A party line. She shares a phone line with several households. It's the most affordable way to have a phone in your house."

Alexa blinked back as she muttered, "No way."

"I hope I've been helpful. I really don't know all that much about Louise's m-murder. I hope you can find the killer, and again, I'm so sorry for your loss, Detective Starr." Mrs. Kinsley unlocked the front door, opened it, then unlocked the screen.

"Thank you, ma'am." Bobby opened his coat and took something from the inside pocket. He held a small card out to Mrs. Kinsley. "Here's my card. If you think of anything else, or if you need us, call that number," he said, then stepped through the screen door onto the porch.

Alexa was about to follow Bobby through the doorway when she paused and turned. "Mrs. Kinsley, was anything missing from Louise when they found her body?"

Mrs. Kinsley's watery blue eyes grew wide. "Why, yes. She always wore her birthstone ring that her father gave her for her sixteenth birthday. She adored her father and the ring was so *special* to her. It was a peridot, a green stone. That's the stone for August. But she wasn't wearing the ring when they found her body. They searched the area for it, but it never turned up. Funny, she was still wearing her cross around her neck, but the ring was gone." She drew in a haggard breath. "I wonder if the killer took it. Not bad enough that they had to kill her, but they took something very precious from her too."

Alexa's heart broke for the woman. She gently cupped her shoulder. "I am so very sorry this has happened to you, Mrs. Kinsley. Please know, we are trying our best to find the person responsible."

When Alexa caught up with Bobby standing near his Chevy she asked, "Do you have a phone? The only phone I saw was the pay phone in the hallway. Please, tell me I overlooked a phone in your apartment."

He shrugged. "Someone always answers, Mrs. Murphy, or one of the Mulaney girls. They'll take a message."

"You take this detective business way too casually, Bobby."

"Maybe." Subtly, he hitched his chin toward something across the street. "Don't make it obvious that you're lookin', but that handsome handyman who's so *dependable* is watchin' us." With that, he touched Alexa's elbow to shepherd her up the sidewalk.

Furtively, she managed a sideways glance. John Hermann was leaning against a telephone pole lighting a cigarette, his toolbox set at his feet. Smoke burst from the tip once the match lit the tobacco. He shook the match fiercely, then tossed it into the gutter. Through the grayish miasma, he watched them progress up the sidewalk. Alexa couldn't take her eyes off him, and it had nothing to do with his good looks. Just then, their eyes locked. She knew she should look away, but instead her gaze clung to his. Who was going to look away first? Finally, she had no choice but to drop the game. She was too far up the street. Something gave Alexa the chills about John Hermann, and she didn't like it.

"I THINK LOUISE MAY HAVE BEEN seeing someone, although she wouldn't admit to it. I was surprised because we'd been friends for so long, and she always told me everything." Marion Hill was an overtly tall, overtly skinny woman who wore her dark tresses scraped back in a bun at the nape of her neck. She reminded Alexa of that silly, clumsy character, Olive Oyl, from the vintage Popeye cartoons. Try as she might, she couldn't get that image out of her head. It wasn't helping that Marion was wearing a red cardigan sweater and a white blouse, buttoned to her throat, adorned with a lace collar. Alexa wondered if anyone had pointed out the resemblance to Marion, being that it was 1953 and Popeye was a popular cartoon on the pages of every newspaper.

"Is it possible she was seeing a married man?" Alexa asked.

Marion swept an errant strand of dark hair from her cheek. Around a careworn sigh, she replied, "I don't think so. I hope not." She whispered, "God, I hope not."

"What do you know about John Hermann?" It was a brazen question that made even Bobby flinch, but she was getting some bad juju from the man, and she wanted to see what Marion's reaction would be.

"John? The handyman?" Planting her left hand on her lean hip while scrubbing her forehead with the fingers from her right, Marion walked in a tight, thoughtful circle. She came to an abrupt halt. "Not everyone knows, but he *is* married. He does a lot of small household maintenance for the widows in the Pittsburgh area. Not just widows, he's been here a time or two. In fact, he was here last Friday. My gutter came loose on the side of the house.

I know Sarah would've loved for John and Louise to get together, but the moment she found out he was married, she backed away from those ideas right away."

Alexa dared another bold question. "Does John see women outside of his marriage?"

A shrug. "I've heard rumors, yes. And in my experience, there's always a kernel of truth to a rumor. But I would hope that Louise wouldn't have fallen into that pit of vipers."

"The night she was killed. The paper stated that you said she went out the back door of the Stanley to avoid the crowds waiting for Peggy Lee. So, was that an unusual exit plan for Louise?"

"Well...yes. We usually went out the side door together, then we'd catch the bus home across the street. Why she decided to go out the back—I wish she hadn't done that." She tried to choke back a whimper but failed. She cupped her hand over her mouth, and through her fingers, she muttered, "She'd still be here now."

Alexa laid a comforting hand on Marion's wrist. "I'm sorry. Just one more question. Was Louise wearing a birthstone ring that night?"

"Louise always wore her birthstone ring. I don't think she ever took it off. For that matter, I'm not sure she could get it off, even if she wanted to. It was very tight. Why are you asking?"

"It wasn't on her body when they found her."

Marion gasped. "That dirty ba—" She took a deep breath. "I'm sorry."

"No need. We understand," Bobby grimly stated.

She crossed the foyer toward Alexa, lifted her right

hand, and stroked a ruby solitaire. "It's funny. You think that if you keep something with you at all times, it will be safe. I wear my mother's engagement ring. It's a pigeon blood ruby. I had it appraised several years back. It's worth ten thousand dollars. I *never* remove it from my hand, but now I have to wonder, is it really safe there?"

Alexa admired the large, round, brilliant red ruby. The gemstone was secured by four raised prongs. "It's a beautiful ring, Marion. I'm sure it's safe. Louise's ring could've come dislodged for many reasons." She felt it was a lie, but it was a kind lie, nonetheless.

"Is there anything else you can tell us about Louise or the night she died?" Bobby asked.

Like, Louise got a cell phone call or a text message? Alexa found herself thinking. Wouldn't that be helpful, but unfortunately, not possible. It was becoming abundantly clear that the detectives of her time had a greater advantage over these poor saps. Sure, they had fingerprinting capabilities in 1953, but nowadays, CSIs provided so much DNA evidence, and crime scenes were handled with kid-gloves care as to not contaminate the area. Little wonder so many murder cases went unsolved back in the day.

Marion eased down onto the second step of the staircase, the outline of her lanky knees protruding under the fabric of her black slacks. Clearly, she was running the evening of May 27th through her mind.

Taking both Alexa and Bobby by surprise, Marion jumped up from the step. "Wait a minute. John Hermann!" Her eyes searched the floor as if she were seeing the man in the woodwork. "How could I have not put this together? John was at the Stanley the night Louise was killed."

Bobby exchanged glances with Alexa, and then he interjected, "A lot of people go to the Stanley, Miss Hill. Maybe he likes Peggy Lee's music."

"No. I saw him talking with Louise in the hallway just beyond the lobby as the crowds were leaving. I was coming down the staircase, and I *saw* them. He was waving his hands around, and she seemed very upset. They were arguing. What could they have been fighting about? I didn't think she knew him well enough to even have a conversation with him. How could I have dismissed it?"

Alexa took her arm and helped ease her back onto the step. "Okay, let's calm down. What happened next?"

Marion's breaths were rapid, panicked. "Louise turned and marched through the lobby, *away* from John. By the time she passed the stairs, I was almost to the bottom. I yelled for her to meet me at the side door. And she yelled that she was going out the back, not to wait for her. I...I never saw her again, not alive anyway."

"Do you remember what John did after their conversation ended?" Alexa asked.

"I saw him go out the front door."

"Was he with anyone, like his wife?" Bobby asked.

"I didn't see anyone with him." Her head jerked up. She gasped. "I should've told the police. They need to know that she was fighting with John Hermann! I'll bet he went around to the back of the theater and strangled her!" She jumped to her feet. "I need to call the police right away!"

"Whoa, whoa, slow down," Bobby said. "Mr. Hermann went out the front, there were loads of people around. I don't think we should accuse him of anything until we have more information. I think we should talk to Mr. Hermann first."

A shiver skittered up Alexa's spine. John Hermann's intense stare from a short time ago played heavy on her mind. His casual lean against the phone pole, the haze of smoke rising like an evil halo above his head, and the way he shook the match until its flame relented. What lurked behind those engaging good looks? If he did kill Louise Kinsley, did he also kill Cora Lee? Again, what was the link between the two women?

As they stepped away from Marion's porch, Bobby asked, "What's so special about that ruby that makes it worth so much? It looked like any ol' ruby to me."

"The pigeon blood is the most sought-after color of the ruby gemstone. That particular stone was large and, as far as I could see without a jeweler's loupe, it was flawless."

"How do you know so much about it?"

"My mom spent several years working for a jeweler. She taught me a lot about gems."

"I'M SORRY ABOUT YOUR WIFE, Mr. Starr. She was a lovely and talented woman. I had the pleasure of hearing her sing at the Hound several times," Ray Howell said, as he gestured for Alexa and Bobby to take seats in his office at the *Pittsburgh Daily Times*. He smiled at Alexa. He was a handsome man. Alexa had him figured right around thirty-eight. Trim, with an athletic build. His dark gray suit was custom made and fit him beautifully. He didn't strike Alexa as a man who would wear anything that wasn't properly fitted. His voice was smooth and confident, and his eyes were filled with intelligence and, like her customer from the twenty-first century, Hayden Mann, a newsman's inquisitiveness. "May I ask who you are, young lady?"

"I'm Alexa Owl, a friend of Mr. Starr's."

"Nice to meet you, Miss Owl." He sank into a black leather chair behind his desk. "What can I do for you today? Are you here to see if I've uncovered any new information on your wife's murder? I know how it is to scrounge for information. Slater won't talk. Most likely because he hasn't got anything."

"Actually, we're here to ask about two murders you covered in the past six months, Cora Lee's and a Louise Kinsley," Alexa said.

He quirked an eyebrow. "Both were quite tragic." He leaned his elbows on the desk, steepled his fingers beneath his chin. "I strongly believe the two murders are connected. Slater won't say."

"I do as well, Mr. Howell," Alexa said.

He smiled, then leaned back. "You have a vested interest in this investigation, Mr. Starr. I'm a reporter who wants exclusive rights to a breaking story. Let's work together to see if we can't break this wide open. I get the story. You get the person responsible for your wife's death. We should exchange information, then we can move forward more quickly."

Alexa's gaze flicked to Bobby. He leaned back, folding his arms over his chest. "What've ya got?"

Ray opened the lower desk drawer on the right and dragged out a file. He spread it open on his desk, then, laying his forearms on the desk, he folded his hands. "Both women, your wife and Miss Kinsley, were strangled. The coroner indicated that both were most likely strangled with a belt of some sort, because of the lack of rope burns on either woman's throat. Miss Kinsley was single, Cora Lee was married, of course." He looked up at Alexa and Bobby with hooded eyes. "I'm not sure if the killer knew the women or if they were simply in the wrong place at the wrong time. However, Mr. Starr, you should talk with your former mother-in-law." He glanced at a framed photograph of a lovely redhead on his desk. She was wearing a white silk blouse with the most impressive ruby necklace. He must've paid a fortune for the piece. "My wife, Susan, and I were at her shop the other day, and she told us that she uses a handyman named John Hermann to do some repairs around the shop. She told Susan she uses him all the time. He's affordable, that sort of thing. Anyway, she was thinking about hiring him for some things we could use done around our house."

"What about it?" Bobby asked.

Closing the file, Ray leaned back, shuffled in his seat. "I'm a reporter, Mr. Starr. Much like yourself, I investigate things. Seems this Louise Kinsley's mother has employed the same man to do repairs around her home as well. I have to wonder if he had eyes for Louise and possibly your wife."

Alexa leaned forward in her chair, about to speak, when Bobby laid a hushing hand on her wrist. Ray's eyes cut to Alexa, then back to Bobby when he said, "Yeah, I'll check into that right away. Got anything else?"

"That's all, for now. Let me know what *you* come up with. We'll trade information in a day or so. Does that sound acceptable?"

"Yeah, sure, why not?" Bobby pushed up from his seat and hitched his chin for Alexa to follow.

"How can I contact you?"

"*I'll* contact you," Bobby said.

When they stepped onto the sidewalk along Grant Street, Alexa asked, "Why didn't you let me tell him about the missing rings?"

Pressing his hands into the pockets of his coat as he started down the sidewalk, Bobby replied, "I don't trust reporters."

"Mr. Howell seems very interested in these two murders."

"Of course he is. If he has more information than we do, and I'm thinking he might, he's not willing to share it. But he wants us to do all the work to confirm his information and get more, so he can have a big front-page headline."

"So what? He gets his headline; we get Cora Lee's murder solved. Win-win."

"I don't trust him."

"We've got to trust someone, Bobby. We've only got *two days* left."

"I gotta get the car back. I'm probably done drinkin' beer by now," Bobby put in as he crossed the street.

Chapter Ten

Pigeon Blood

Bobby managed to park the Chevy about one spot closer to the pub. He turned the ignition off. The car rattled, most likely thankful to be back at rest. He tossed the keys under the mat, then sat staring at the steering wheel for several moments. Alexa could tell his contemplation was troubling. Finally, he looked up through the windshield at the soft flurry now falling. "Wait for me inside the Hound. But don't go up to the apartment. I might be there."

"Where are you going?" Alexa asked.

He didn't look at her. Instead, he studied the snowflakes touching down on the hood of the car, melting away instantly. "Howell said I should talk with Anna, right? It's a lead, right? I'm gonna follow that lead. The shop is a half block or so down the Strip, and I don't think it's a good idea for me to show up with a strange woman. She's been through so much. First George, then Cora, and Frank."

Alexa snorted. "I'm not *that* strange."

"*That's* a matter of opinion." Bobby's voice was playful, but she was proud of him. He was taking his former mother-in-law's heartbreak into account.

The car door let out a wheeze of agony as Bobby shouldered it open and an even louder objection when he slammed it closed hard enough that it clicked on the first attempt. Jamming his hands into the pockets of his coat, he hunkered deeper into the collar as he slowly made his way along Penn Avenue. Alexa watched him go until he disappeared into a clutch of shoppers hurrying along the Strip. Holiday shopping was in full swing, and she felt badly for those whose Christmas wouldn't be so bright this year—Sarah Kinsley, Anna Baker, Marion Hill—and though he was good at veiling his despair, Bobby was feeling it too.

Not really in the mood to hang out at the Hound, Alexa decided to take a walk up the Strip, check out some of the holiday décor, maybe visit some of the shops from yesteryear. That should be an interesting way to spend an hour or so. She grabbed the handle to open the door, but the car door would not budge. She pushed and shoved to no avail. Finally, she pressed her heels against the floor just under the seat for more leverage, when she felt something tumble between her feet. Letting go of the handle, she looked down to find a handgun on the floor. She couldn't believe it. Who would leave a gun in their vehicle parked along a main street? It was one thing for Bobby to leave his car keys under the mat, but this was a gun, for crying out loud.

Carefully, Alexa took up the gun. Whoa. Talk about old film noir. She was holding a Colt Detective Special.

Many police detectives carried a gun such as this back in the day, but it was the film industry of the forties and fifties that put this baby on the map. Every Hollywood detective was carrying a handgun just like the one in her grip. And there it was, engraved in the side plate: Colt Detective Special. She popped open the cylinder—it was loaded! Stunned, she slammed the cylinder shut, took up her purse and put the gun inside. What in God's name was wrong with Bobby, leaving a loaded gun in an unlocked car? With frustration on her side, she shouldered the door hard and it opened. She practically fell out of the vehicle onto the sidewalk. Managing to regain her balance, she smoothed her coat, then, with the heel of her shoe, she kicked the door closed. A walk up the avenue would do her some good. At this point, she needed to cool off, but Bobby was absolutely going to hear about this.

TAKING IN A BRACED BREATH, Bobby pressed through the door of his former in-laws' shoe shop. His father-in-law, Frank Baker, had passed away about two weeks after Cora's death. Heart attack. Anna claimed he died of a broken heart. Their oldest child, George, had been killed in a car accident four years before. Anna had been through so much, and now *he* was showing up at the shop. As sweet and kind and loving as Anna was, he doubted she'd be happy to see him. Frank did not approve of Cora's marriage to the private detective. Frank considered him a failure, loser, not worth his daughter's hand, and Bobby couldn't blame him. Now he had a chance to make things right—to bring Cora's murderer to justice, and with any luck, Louise Kinsley's too.

"Bobby!" Anna's voice cried out. Much to his surprise, her tone was pleasant. He looked up to see her coming toward him with a smile on her lips—Cora's smile and the same caring, sweet eyes too. She enveloped him in a hug. "I'm so glad to see you. It's been a long time. I don't think you've dropped by since...well, since Cora's funeral."

"I've been busy. How are you?" It was the most he could manage when she released the embrace.

Anna hooked her arm in his. "I'm doing as well as can be expected. It's lonely without Frank and Cora. The house seemed way too big and way too quiet when Cora left. It's much worse now." She escorted him past an employee with a smoldering cigarette dangling from his lip while tapping at the sole of a woman's shoe at a workbench near the far wall. "You remember Martin Fitch, don't you, Bobby?"

The man looked up with hooded eyes and nodded. "Mate."

Bobby nodded his greeting in return. He remembered seeing Martin in the pub just yesterday when he and Alexa had arrived. At the time, he couldn't remember his name, though he did recall the guy was never particularly friendly. Immediately Bobby's eyes cut to Frank's workbench, which stood not far from Martin's. Frank's bench had been closed up; it was obvious it hadn't been used in quite some time. Anna held back a heavy, dark blue curtain and Bobby stepped through into a small back room where a tiny kitchen and Anna's sewing machine were located. Several dresses and a man's suit hung on a rack on the far wall behind her machine stationed near the back door that led into the alley.

Anna gestured for him to have a seat at the small kitchenette. "Can I get you something to eat or drink?"

That was Anna. Kind to everyone. Bobby had no idea if she approved of his marriage to her daughter or not. Anna was always so benevolent to everyone, no matter their station in life.

He eased into a chair. "No, thank you, Anna."

She pulled open the door to the fridge and peered inside. "Are you sure? I've got several Stoney's in the back of the fridge." Bobby shook his head no. She closed the door. Her voice was soft. "It was Frank's favorite beer. He and Martin would sit at this table every night after we closed, and they'd drink a Stoney's before we'd head for home. Did you know, the daughter of the man who owns the brewery, what's her name? Shirley...Shirley Jones. Anyway, she won that Miss Pittsburgh contest last summer. That nice man from the paper was here the other day. He said he's set up a big interview with her later this week. He seemed quite excited about it." She slipped into the chair across the table.

"Ray Howell?"

"Yes, that's his name."

Martin pressed through the curtain and made his way to the coffee pot sitting on the small stove next to the refrigerator.

"Why was Ray Howell here? Was he asking questions about Cora?"

"He was here with his wife. I'm doing a few alterations on a dress for her," Anna supplied.

"I spoke with Mr. Howell not long ago. He said you've been using a handyman named John Hermann." Bobby kept an eye on Martin as he stirred sugar into his coffee mug, then lingered near the stove.

"Yes, he does a good job and he's dependable. I've been using his services ever since Cora told me about him when we were having trouble with this sink." She gestured to a small sink next to the refrigerator. "In fact, he was here just yesterday. Frank was always so busy."

Martin turned to lean a hip against the stove. "I don't trust the man. Seems he preys on women who have no men around. That's what I think."

Anna waved a careless hand. "Oh, Martin. You're just too protective. John's a very nice man."

"So, Cora knew John Hermann?" Bobby inquired.

Anna lifted her right shoulder, then let it drop. "I don't think she *knew* him. She knew *of* him. I don't think they were friends. She said he'd come into that pub every once in a while, when she was singing. Mr. Howell seemed interested in him too. His wife, Susan, asked how much he charged for his services. Mr. Howell was very interested in a pair of shoes Martin was making, *alligator* shoes. He went into the showroom with Martin to see them, while I was looking at Susan's hem. He might do a story for the *Times* about our shop. Isn't that exciting?"

Bobby glanced sideways at Martin. "Sure is."

"Why are you asking about John? Has he done something wrong?"

"I don't know," Bobby said.

"Wouldn't surprise me none," Martin mumbled, then took a sip of his coffee.

Alexa strolled along the shops of the Strip District, taking in the sights and the smells. She was anxious to hear what Bobby found out from his former mother-in-law. Maybe he was back by now. So, she decided to turn around to head toward the Lazy Hound when she almost plowed into a woman coming out of the Wholesale Cheese Company.

"Excuse me! I'm so sorry. I wasn't paying—" Alexa began. The woman turned and she found herself face to face with Catherine.

"I just can't get away from you, can I?" Catherine groused. She looked around. "Where's Bobby? Oh, dear, are you left not knowing where he is *again*? Maybe he's not as taken with you as you think."

Alexa let out a contemptuous guffaw. "Gee whiz, Catherine, he evidently hasn't been all that thrilled with you. I mean, he *married* Cora Lee, didn't he?"

"I don't know what Bobby saw in Cora Lee, other than she was a singer and her parents have money—"

Another opportunity to stir the pot or, in Catherine's case, a cauldron. "Don't forget pretty. I saw a picture. Cora Lee was quite the beauty."

Catherine puffed up like an agitated hen protecting her peeps. "Listen to me, whoever you *think* you are. I love Bobby. I was *supposed* to marry Bobby, and then *she* came along. And now you. Well, I'm warning you right now, I'm not putting up with it. I don't know what you want with my Bobby, but you mark my words, I'm going to get him back! One way or the other." Catherine was an expert stomper and that's exactly what she did, she stomped away.

Don't worry, honey. You'll have your chance. As fleeting as it may be, you'll have your chance.

Suddenly, Catherine spun around. "Oh, and by the way, Bobby spent time with me while he was married to Cora Lee. So, it's not like he was a faithful husband to her. Guess that's why she was cheating on him. *Hm*?" With that, she exercised her stomping skills once again.

Now Alexa had to wonder if they were looking in the right direction. Maybe Cora Lee and Louise Kinsley's murders weren't connected at all. Maybe the two killings looked alike, but, in fact, were totally separate. Was it possible that Catherine murdered Cora Lee out of rage and spite?

Sirens tore through the din of the Strip District. Alexa looked up to see a police car racing down the avenue. As it passed by, she glimpsed Detective Clifton Slater in the passenger seat. She didn't know what had happened, but it looked pretty serious. She took note of the police car's number: 32.

Wait. What did Catherine just say? Bobby had cheated on Cora Lee with her? What was wrong with that man? A loaded gun left in an unlocked car and cheating on his wife with that dragon lady? Now she was stomping along the sidewalk toward the pub. She had a few choice things to say to Mr. Bobby Starr!

Alexa hesitated for a moment. Bobby's old clunker was still parked along the curb. That meant the Bobby from 1953 was somewhere near. That wasn't the Bobby she was looking for, although he was just as guilty. She jerked the door to the pub open, looked across the large room. Winnie was in her usual spot, at the end of the bar, poring over homework. No Bobby.

"Excuse me, miss," Molly Mulaney's voice broke through her irritation. "Aren't you Mr. Starr's friend?" she asked, as she set down two beers on a table in front of a couple. She looked tired, haggard, and careworn.

"'Friend' is a loose description of our relationship, but yes," Alexa stated.

Molly hurried toward her, slipping something from the pocket of her yellow apron. "Me daughter, Maggie, brought this downstairs a few minutes ago. She said she knocked on Mr. Starr's door, but he didn't answer." She held out a note toward Alexa. "A woman called and left this message for him. Can you see to it that he gets it?"

"Maggie said the woman was upset. She said she thinks it's all about Cora Lee." Winnie was suddenly standing next to her mother, gazing up at Alexa with anticipation filling her big, brown eyes.

Molly planted her hands on her hips. "You'll be mindin' your own business and your *homework*, Wynona Mulaney." She pointed adamantly toward the discarded homework lying on the bar. Shoulders drooping, Winnie shuffled toward the dreaded school assignments. She shot a dirty look at her older sister, Maggie, who was busy taking the couple's order. Molly followed her youngest daughter.

Alexa unfolded the note. The message was scribbled but legible.

Something bad is happening at Marion Hill's house
Come quickly! Sarah Kinsley

If she had her cell phone, she could call Mrs. Kinsley or Bobby, but Alexa didn't have time to dwell on what was not possible. Taking a few swift steps toward the door, she paused. Maybe she should have Molly or Maggie tell Bobby where she was going. She turned and took one step, then retreated. Wait, they might tell the wrong Bobby, then the wrong Bobby could show up at Marion's and make a mess of things that may be a mess already. No. She was on her own, and she needed to get to Mrs. Kinsley's house immediately. Alexa didn't have the convenience of a cell phone, but there was an old Chevy parked right outside, and she knew exactly where the keys were. Tucking the note into her coat pocket, she darted out the door.

WHEN ALEXA MADE THE RIGHT TURN onto Cresson Street, she was shocked to see the police had most of it blocked off. Flashing lights sliced through the afternoon snow and bluster. Police officers milled about near their cruisers lined up in front of Marion's house. Alexa parked the car along the curb in front of Sarah Kinsley's house, then sat for several minutes watching the chaos. There it was—car 32. Detective Slater was on the case.

Alexa scanned Cresson Street. Neighbors were huddled close along the length of the sidewalk, pointing and gaping at the unsettling activity at the Hill residence. Sarah Kinsley stood at the edge of her porch wearing a winter coat that was two or three sizes too big. One hand cupped over her mouth, she was clearly beside herself, overwrought with worry.

Giving a hefty heave-ho, Alexa slammed her shoulder against the door, and, to the delight of her already sore shoulder, the car door scraped open. Only this time she held onto the steering wheel as to not fall out of the vehicle. She dropped the keys onto the floor, then draped her purse over her forearm. It was much heavier with the gun inside.

The moment Alexa made purchase with the sidewalk, she heard Mrs. Kinsley calling out to her. "Miss Owl! I'm so glad you're here. Something dreadful has happened to Marion." Just then a white panel van with the words Allegheny County Coroner in large black print on the side rolled past. Mrs. Kinsley gasped. "Oh, no, something worse than dreadful."

Alexa climbed the four steps onto the porch to wrap a comforting arm around Mrs. Kinsley. She was shivering, and Alexa was certain it had more to do with the woman's anxiety than the icy weather. "Why don't you go inside, Mrs. Kinsley? Make a cup of tea. I'm going to walk up to Marion's house and see what I can find out. Okay?"

Tears streaming down her pale cheeks, Mrs. Kinsley could only manage a nod. Alexa walked her to the door, then made her way across the porch, down the steps, and headed straight for Marion Hill's house. Only, how was she going to gain access to the crime scene? Her mother always said if you look like you belong, act like you belong, no one will question whether or not you belong. With that somewhat dicey advice in mind, she set a confident expression on her face and in her stride. She just hoped none of the police officers witnessed her arrive in that contraption Bobby called a car.

The policemen and the medics didn't give her a second glance as she strolled past them and climbed the steps that led to Marion's front porch. An officer coming out of the front door smiled and held the door open for her as she stepped inside. Well, that was easy enough. A throng of activity urged her to peer into the living room, and the sight made her gasp.

Marion's motionless body lay on the floor. An older man hovered over her, examining her. Alexa couldn't believe what she was seeing. The man had a cigarette in his mouth, as did many of the police officers milling about the room. One officer tossed his cigarette to the floor, crushing it with his heel. She was stunned at the sheer lack of concern for a crime scene. While she was no CSI or crime expert of any kind, she knew for certain they were contaminating literally *everything*.

"What are you doing here?" Detective Slater's voice made her flinch. She turned. He craned his neck to peer past her shoulder. "Where's your boyfriend?"

Alexa crossed her arms. The gun inside her purse clunked against her side. "He's *not* my boyfriend."

"You took my advice. That's a relief." His tone was as dry as dust.

"He's *never* been my boyfriend. Thank you very much."

He shot her an odd look. "Um, you're welcome. What are you doing here, Miss Owl?"

"Marion was a friend." Now, she was really going to go out on a limb. "What happened?"

"She was strangled."

How could that be? She and Bobby had been in this

very house, talking with this very woman, mere hours ago.

"Strangled, like Louise Kinsley and Cora..." From the corner of her eye she thought she saw Ray Howell walk past.

"Yes, Miss Kinsley and Mrs. Starr were strangled, but this murder is much different," he said. Alexa stretched to look around bodies in the way. *Was that Ray Howell?* Detective Slater glanced about the room. "What are you looking for?"

"Is Ray Howell here?"

"Unfortunately, yes. He was the one who called the police. He said he had an appointment to talk with Miss Hill and when he arrived, he found her dead. Why?"

"May I see the body?" Alexa asked. It was a long shot, but hey, she'd come this far.

"That works. You can confirm her identity for the coroner, since you were *friends*," Slater said.

The way he emphasized the word *friends* gave her the impression he wasn't buying her story. No matter, she was getting a shocking opportunity to check something out. In fact, the entire murder scene was shocking. After all, she had just waltzed through the front door as if she were a welcomed guest. In her time, she wouldn't have gotten within twenty feet of the door, friend or not. She had to wonder if Cliff exchanged police stories with his grandfather, that is, if Clifton Slater was still among the living. If so, wouldn't he be amazed how stringently murder scenes were handled in the future...er...nowadays... um...hereafter...ah...currently—*whatever*.

"Miss Owl..."

She blinked and realized he'd been trying to get her attention for a moment or so. She asked, "Why do I need to identify Marion? Didn't Mr. Howell do that?"

Slater shrugged. "Howell said he was fairly sure the woman is Miss Hill, but he couldn't be absolutely positive. After all, he claimed he only interviewed her once on a rather dark sidewalk, near the Stanley Theater, the night Miss Kinsley died."

"That makes sense, I suppose," she said.

He led her into the living room. Her gaze momentarily met Ray's. Pen and pad in hand, Ray looked away quickly to continue talking with an officer. When they approached the coroner, he stood and waved to his assistant, who immediately came forward to cover Marion's body with a white sheet.

Slater said, "Bill, I've got someone who says she can identify the body." The coroner turned to study Alexa with a guarded gaze. "This is Alexa Owl, she's a *friend* of Miss Hill's."

There was that inflection on the word *friend* again. Was she really that bad of a liar? Her mother always said that a lie scalded her cheeks red, and at the moment her face did feel a bit warm, but how could Slater know her mother's secret?

"Uncover her face," the coroner instructed the assistant.

Alexa wasn't quite prepared to look into the ashen, lifeless face of Marion Hill. She let out a gasp before she could call it back, absently drawing her fingers to her lips. Closing her eyes, she slid her hand to her chest, nodded, then quietly managed, "Yes, that's Marion Hill." She opened her eyes in time to see the billow of the sheet as the assistant draped it over Marion's face. "Wait. I need to see one more thing."

The coroner and Detective Slater's brows furrowed. The assistant paused, looking to his boss for a directive. The coroner inquired, "What do you want to see, Miss Owl?"

She swallowed hard. At this juncture, Alexa was pretty darn sure she was overstepping boundaries, but she had to know, and she had to point it out if her suspicion proved correct. "I need to see her right hand. I'm pretty sure it's her right hand."

The coroner and Detective Slater exchanged ambiguous glances. Slater asked, "Why?"

"Marion wore a ring. It was a valuable pigeon blood ruby. She claimed that she never took the ring off because it had belonged to her mother. I want to see if it's still on her hand or if the killer took it."

Again, the coroner and the detective exchanged questioning looks. The assistant waited, poised for instruction. Finally, the coroner nodded his approval, and the sheet was swept back to reveal Marion's body down to her hands—her bare hands. The coroner's eyes snapped toward Alexa. "You're absolutely sure she wore a ruby ring?"

"Absolutely."

The coroner gestured for his assistant to cover Marion's body, then waved the medics forward to lift her onto the gurney. He closed his bag and headed for the door. "See ya later, Cliff."

"See ya, Bill." Detective Slater spun around toward a clutch of officers across the room. "Ben, go upstairs into Miss Hill's bedroom. You're looking for a ruby ring. Someone check the kitchen and the bathroom." The officers immediately trotted out of the room. Heavy footsteps could be heard on the stairs as two climbed. One officer made his way toward the kitchen.

"Detective, Sarah Kinsley told me Louise wore a birthstone ring and that it was missing from her body. Marion said that the ring was so tight on Louise's finger that she couldn't get it off—"

"Yes. I'm aware of the missing jewelry from each victim. The killer broke Louise's finger in order to remove her ring," Slater explained.

Absently, Alexa thought out loud. "So, the rings must be some kind of a trophy for the killer..."

"A *what*?" Slater asked.

Suddenly, the sound of the gurney's wheels moving toward her caught Alexa's attention. she took several steps to get out of the way, only to feel a sharp stab in her big toe. "Ouch!" Hopping on her right foot, she reached down to slip the pump from her left.

Slater grabbed her by the arm to steady her. "Are you okay?"

"I stepped on something, and I think it poked through my shoe," Alexa said. Her brows furrowed as she tipped the shoe forward to examine the toe. Sure enough, a tiny nail protruded the sole. She turned the shoe over. The nail hadn't gone all the way through. It was small with a flat head. She tugged and twisted the nail out of the leather and held it up.

Slater's eyes narrowed. "Where did that come from?"

"It sure is tiny," Alexa noted. "I wonder what it's from."

"I can't be sure," Slater replied.

"They always leave *something* behind," she muttered to herself.

"Excuse me?"

"Nothing. May I keep this?"

He shrugged. "I don't see why not."

Alexa carefully placed the nail in the cool little red velvet change purse with a twist-snap closure. Retro or vintage to her, in style to those around her currently.

"If the officer doesn't find the ring upstairs, I have a theory of another place you might find it." Ray Howell's announcement made Alexa and Slater turn. Clearly their steadfast interest in his supposition warmed the cockles of his little newsman's heart.

"Let's have it," Detective Slater said.

"A friend told me a local handyman was keeping a ring in his toolbox. He said he saw the guy with the ring. I saw this man walking down Cresson when I arrived. His name is John Hermann. You might want to talk with him," Ray said.

Chapter Eleven

Stick to It

On her drive back to the pub, Alexa felt it was time to review what she knew: Louise Kinsley was a single woman who had little money. She was strangled, late at night, behind a popular theater. Her birthstone ring was stolen. Her mother, Sarah Kinsley, used John Hermann as a handyman.

Cora Lee Starr was a married woman who came from wealth. She was a singer in a pub and was strangled late at night behind said pub. Her wedding ring was stolen. Allegedly, her mother, Anna Baker, employed John Hermann as a handyman, although Bobby had yet to confirm that information. However, Cora Lee also had an adversary—Catherine Campbell, Bobby's future third wife. As far as Alexa knew, neither of the other two women had enemies. Catherine struck her as an unscrupulous, resourceful woman.

Alexa had to wonder, could Catherine have waited behind the Lazy Hound for Cora Lee, snuck up from behind, and strangled her in the name of vexed love for Bobby? Could she have taken Cora Lee's wedding band as a deranged trophy and used it as fodder to accuse Cora Lee as an unfaithful wife? Far-fetched? Maybe. Possible? Yep, and certainly an avenue worth exploring. Besides, it might be fun to rattle Catherine's chain a bit.

Never mind that. On to the next...

Marion Hill was a single woman who seemed to be on the comfortable side of finances. It appeared her parents had seen to that. She was strangled in her home in the middle of the afternoon, a slightly different M.O. from the other two victims. She admitted to using John Hermann's services as well, and now, after a search of her home, it had been determined Marion's pigeon blood ruby ring was missing.

All three women shared three common denominators—each was strangled, each had a ring stolen from their body, and each woman knew or used John Hermann's handyman services.

The moment it was decided Marion's ruby ring could possibly be missing, Ray Howell stepped forward to point an accusing finger at John Hermann. Ray stated that he'd seen John walking along Cresson Street as he was arriving. Furthermore, someone had told him he saw John with a ring in his toolbox. Detective Slater wasted no time. He was presently on his way to question the handyman. Alexa had considered telling the detective about the argument Marion had witnessed between Louise and John Hermann at the Stanley Theater the night she was murdered. Instead she decided to sit on the information for a little while longer.

And then there was the nail she'd stepped on in Marion's living room. It was such a tiny nail. Where had it come from? The more she contemplated the nail, she had to wonder, was it a shoemaker's nail? If so, had it fallen out of one of Marion's shoes? Had she recently had a pair of shoes repaired? Unlike the twentieth century, shoe repair and shoemaker shops were abundant in the 1950s. Marion could've had a shoe repaired in a variety of places around town, including Baker's Shoes.

After what seemed like forever, Alexa was steering the old hunk of junk to the curb near the Lazy Hound. A plume of ashen smoke circling his head, Bobby was pacing up and down the sidewalk in front of the pub. He looked rife with agitation. Well, she would've texted him to let him know where she was, *if* cell phones had been invented. One thing was for sure, she'd never take technology for granted again. Bobby's head jerked up when the car door cried out for mercy as she shouldered it open. He tossed his cigarette into the gutter, then jogged toward her.

"Where the hell have you been?" Bobby demanded.

"Now, now, Detective Starr. I don't think Pete would appreciate that kind of language."

He blew out a frustrated breath. "Sorry, where've you been?"

"I've been to Marion Hill's home. She was strangled this afternoon. I spoke with your friends, Detective Slater and Ray Howell. Remember the pigeon blood ruby?" Bobby nodded. "Well, the murderer took it from her body. Howell accused John Hermann, and Detective Slater is questioning him now."

"Oh, Slater's doin' more than questioning the dependable handyman. He's been arrested for murder. A friend of mine from the precinct was in the Hound just a bit ago. He told me they found Louise Kinsley's ring in his toolbox. He's been taken into custody, and of course Ray Howell was right there to get the scoop. I guess we know who killed Cora, Louise, and Marion."

Alexa rolled her eyes. "As Inspector Clouseau would say, let me bring you up to speed. We know *nothing*. Now, you're up to speed."

"Who's Inspector...Closet?"

Alexa shook her head. "Never mind."

Bobby narrowed his eyes. Clearly he was confused. "You say the weirdest things."

She smiled. "Weird is my super power."

Bobby tossed his hands in the air. "And there you go again. What does *that* mean?"

"It means..." She sucked in her lips. "I don't have time for this. No, *you* don't have time for this." She rifled through her purse to come up with the velvet change purse. Gingerly, she poked around inside the sack with her finger searching for the nail. Pinching the nail between her pointer and her thumb, she held it up.

Again, Bobby's expression displayed pure befuddlement. "What are you doing with a shoemaker's nail?"

"I figured you'd know exactly what it was. You get ten points, Starr. Detective Slater couldn't identify it. But the real question is, what was this nail doing near Marion's body? Like I told you before, a murderer always leaves *something* behind."

"You also said it would be something more scientific.

A shoemaker's nail is hardly scientific."

"Oh, don't worry. I'm sure he left something scientific behind. You just don't have the technology to find it. Fact is, we lucked out. He left something physical behind, and I was lucky enough to step on it."

"You don't know that for sure, Alexa. It could've fallen out of one of her shoes. *Fact is*, they found *physical evidence* on John Hermann. Marion told us she saw Louise arguing with him at the Stanley the night she was killed. The guy did odd jobs for all three victims. He knew all three women, maybe not intimately, but he knew them. Fact is, *I lose*. Slater solved Cora's case before I did." He plucked a pack of cigarettes from the inside pocket of his coat, stuffed one in his mouth, then turned to go inside the Lazy Hound while holding a lighter to the tip.

"What a big ol' quitter you are, Starr!" What was she saying? What was she doing? This was her out. This was her opportunity to go back to the twenty-first century and get Bobby Starr out of her life, for good. But it simply didn't feel right. He turned. Only this time his expression wasn't one of bewilderment. This time, he was looking at her with a steely gaze. He marched at her like an angry grizzly bear, and for a moment Alexa thought it might be wise to just shut up. Except, that wasn't who she was. "That's right. You're a *quitter*. That's why Pete required you to solve *three* cases. He didn't believe you'd have the stick-to-it-ness to solve Cora Lee's murder. And boy, oh, boy, looks like he was *right*."

Now he was standing over her, his body rigid as a steel beam. He blew a thick stream of smoke directly into her face. Alexa turned away, hacking. "Let me see that nail," he demanded. Through watering eyes and fits of coughs, she shoved the nail into his hand. "Okay, Owl. What do *you* think we should do?"

Helpless but determined, Alexa leaned against the pub. "We've got more suspects than...*cough*...than Hermann." More coughing. She glanced up and Bobby looked regretful. "I think...*cough*...Ray Howell's presence at Marion's house was too convenient. He seemed to know John Hermann..." Her voice fell away. She cleared her throat. "Ray knew John Hermann would have something in his possession—like the ring. He said someone had told him John had it."

"Who?" Bobby asked.

Without warning, she suddenly felt that downward suction. Oh, no! Not now! She could feel herself slipping away—away from 1953 and Bobby's dilemma. She had one more thing to tell him, "And then there's the nail!"

She heard him cry out before she was gone. "Alexa!"

Bobby needed her. Maybe Pete had other plans.

Chapter Twelve

Time's Ticking Away

I s that you, Alexa? I mean, is that the real you?" Winnie's voice was quiet and apprehensive.

Alexa slowly opened her eyes. Every time she made the transition from 1953 to current time or vice versa, she felt a bit dizzy, dazed, and this time there was a dash of nausea thrown into the mix. She felt as though she'd been driving on a winding road at a high speed with Natalyn at the wheel—*Natalyn*! Grabbing her head, she sat up too fast. "Ugh, I never called Nat back. She's gonna kill me."

She felt Winnie's reassuring touch on her knee. "Your dear sister stopped by. She wasn't happy you hadn't called, but she figured you were very busy." Shaking her head, Winnie sighed. "She has no idea just how busy. She dropped in to let you know there's an offer for your parents' house. The realtor would like you to review the offer and let her know by the weekend. I put the paperwork in the office so Stacia wouldn't set it on fire or worse."

Alexa glanced down. The gold shirt dress with the

Peter Pan collar was gone, replaced with a pair of chocolate leggings, a leopard print off-the-shoulder tunic, and a pair of shiny silver flip-flops. Her hair was drawn up in a messy bun. Her earlobes suddenly felt heavy. She reached up with her right hand to finger a pair of big silver hoops. She slipped the hoops off and tossed them onto the ottoman. Exhaustion was setting in fast. Essentially, she was living two lives—as if one life wasn't complicated enough. Then she felt the pinch from her strapless bra. Alexa was too tired and cranky to deal with that, so she wiggled around until she managed to unhook it, pulled it out from under the tunic, then tossed it to the floor. Satisfied and more comfortable, she sagged back against the sofa, closing her eyes. "So, Stacia isn't working out, I take it."

"She doesn't work here anymore. You let her go after the firemen left," Winnie said.

Alexa jerked up from her relaxed position. "*Firemen!* Oh, dear God! What happened?"

Again, Winnie patted her leg. "It's all right, lass. No one was hurt. But you'll be needin' to call the insurance company. There's a bit of a mess in the little kitchen next to me office. Stacia put a pot on to boil for tea and forgot about it." Draping her right elbow over her eyes, Alexa dropped back against the sofa with a groan. Winnie added, "Now, if you're lookin' for a silver lining, you managed to hire a tailor today."

Instantly, Alexa let her arm drop away from her face. "I did?"

"Mr. Hayden's suit is finished. You just need to pick the buttons. I'll put them on in the morning, and then it'll be ready for pressing. I can't wait to use that old mangle you've got in the back. I've never seen or used one before," a man's baritone voice said from across the room.

Alexa pushed up to look in the direction of that deep voice. Strolling toward her was a breathtakingly handsome man. Square, strong jawline. His black T-shirt clung to a chiseled chest, muscled arms spilled from the sleeves, and his jeans were snug against lean hips. His brown hair was cut close, and his eyes were the color of coffee. Her breath caught. *Whoa.*

Winnie whispered, "Down girl. He's not your type."

Alexa asked out of the side of her mouth, "Says who?"

"Says his boyfriend, most likely."

Her shoulders wilted. "He's gay?" Winnie nodded. Alexa sighed. "All the gorgeous ones are."

He came to the edge of the sofa and leaned his hand on the back. Now, she had a perfect view of just how striking he was. "If there's nothing else for today, I'll be on my way. I need to pick something up for dinner. My night to cook."

"And you cook too?" The words blurted out before she could call them back.

He smiled. "Yeah, I cook. I'll have you over some time. You and Cliff."

Wait...I told him about Cliff? Wow. I'm not usually so forthcoming with strangers.

He bent down closer. "So, am I good to go?"

Alexa cleared her throat, mostly in an attempt to clear her thoughts. "Yes, you're...good."

"See ya tomorrow around nine." He started for

the door, then hesitated at the end of the bar to pluck something from the tray Winnie tended to bring with her every morning, filled with something delectable. He held up what looked like a cookie. "These were great, Winnie, thanks," he said, then tossed the cookie into his mouth. Both Alexa and Winnie watched him walk toward the door, where he paused again and turned. "Hey, sorry about your kitchen. At least the fire was contained in that room." He snorted. "Hope your next salesgirl is more... um...careful." With that, he slipped out the door. Alexa lifted up a bit, craning her neck to watch him through the storefront window. He got into a black BMW, then pulled into traffic—missing the pothole.

Alexa plopped down. "Well, either his former employer paid very well, or his partner is well off."

"What kind of a partner? You only hired one person," Winnie said.

"You said he had a partner."

"I didn't. I said he had a boyfriend."

Alexa chuckled. "Same thing." Winnie's face crinkled a bit. "What? What's that look for?"

"I just hope there's no sobriety tests going on between here and his apartment."

Cocking her head to one side, Alexa apprehensively asked, "And we should be concerned about that, *because...*"

"Oh. Well, he's had quite a few of me cookies, and you know what me favorite ingredient is."

Alexa flopped her head back against the sofa. "Ugh."

"Don't ya want to know his name, then? Just in case you have to post bail for your new tailor."

The corners of Alexa's lips lifted. "I suppose that would be useful information."

"Holden Emery. I rather like it, and he is a handsome lad. Just moved here from New York City about two weeks ago. He was a costume maker for the Majestic Theater. Sounds very...majestic. He told you, the *other* you, he'd rather work in a shop, so he was thrilled to see the sign in the window. He lives in Highland Park. I think he's gonna work out just fine."

"Good to know. But why do you think that?" Alexa inquired.

"About an hour after he was here, you were havin' troubles with Murielle Baker. She wasn't happy with the shade of rose you picked for her dress. Well, he strolled into the dressing room and made such a fuss over how beautiful she looked that I think you could've sold her three more just like it."

"Murielle...did I happen to ask her about Cora Lee?"

"No, but I did. She said she remembered her aunt, and the murder, but her family never spoke of the details. It was all too painful for them," Winnie explained.

Just then, Garbo leapt onto the ottoman. Alexa was taken aback. The beautiful white cat had been translucent from the start, except now, she was fading away. Alexa could see the set of triple full-length mirrors straight through Garbo's midsection. Alexa asked, "What's happening to Garbo?"

"I'm not quite sure. It's almost as if she's disappearin'. You and Bobby have little more than twenty-four hours left to solve Cora Lee's murder. I hope you're gettin' close."

Alexa scrutinized the cat. "Maybe that's what Garbo's trying to tell me."

"Alexa...do ya mind if I ask you something?" Winnie seemed unsure of herself.

Sitting up and turning to face her friend, Alexa said, "Certainly."

"Have you seen me mother and father, or me sisters?"

"Yes, I've seen all of them."

Winnie clapped her hands together. "Ah, it's 1953 and they're all full of life, aren't they?"

Alexa's heart pinched. Yes, they were all alive, but heartache seemed to fill the pub. She wanted to ask Winnie about Ellie. Did her older sister come back? Did Molly and Brian accept Ellie's decision to marry the Jewish man and reconcile with their daughter? She hoped so. But she didn't want to ruin Winnie's fantasy of her parents and her sisters, all alive and well and working at the pub they loved. Instead, she laid her hand on Winnie's leg and smiled. "Yes, they sure are."

Winnie favored her with a bright Irish grin. "Well, I don't have a pint to raise up, but here's to hopin' they were safe and sound in heaven a half hour before the devil knew any of them were dead."

Shaking her head, Alexa chortled. "Oh, Winnie."

A STEADY RAIN HAD FALLEN, and the sky flashed with lightning, cooling the air, washing away the haze and humidity. After the rain had passed, a light breeze swept through the Strip District. Alexa had taken advantage of the waning heat wave to open her bedroom windows for fresh air. It was the wee hours of July 18th when she rolled over and awakened. The curtains blew out in fat billows on the easy waft, then sucked back against the screen. Garbo rested on her perch, keeping watch over the parking lot below. The muted moonlight glittered through her. Indeed, she was diminishing. Was she leaving this world because they were running out of time, or was she trying to tell her *you're on the right track, human*?

Only, Alexa had been removed from the situation, the investigation. She had to wonder if Pete would send her back, or did he feel it was time for Bobby to forge ahead on his own? After all, it was he who had to fulfill the requirements, not her. Alexa's obligation was to *assist* Bobby, and perhaps Pete felt she'd satisfied her part of the bargain. Still, lying in the cool breeze, watching the curtains float in and out, and Garbo's heedful guard, she worried what was going on back there in 1953. John Hermann, Ray Howell, Catherine, and that nail she'd found near Marion's body—thoughts of each whirled through her unsettled, fatigued mind.

On second thought, or maybe five hundred and second thought, was it really possible for Catherine to be the murderer? Out of the three victims, Cora Lee was the only woman Catherine had a beef with. Most likely, she didn't know Louise or Marion. Besides, Bobby actually ended up marrying the dragon lady—that's history. So, if they found Catherine to be the killer, at least Cora Lee's killer, that would change the turn of events. Right? Pete told Bobby that was not to happen. Therefore, that takes Catherine out of the equation, she supposed. Sooo, what history had John Hermann or Ray Howell plotted?

Interesting theory. She was fairly sure she could find the answer.

Slowly, she pushed up from the bed. Garbo turned her head at the movement. "It's okay, kitty. I'm just going to check on something or someone." Garbo dismissed her. No surprise there. In the darkness, she padded down the hallway, pausing at the wall where the pay phone had been stationed all those years ago. Feeling a sudden wave of nostalgia, she ran her hand over the spot, then continued to the living room. The street lamps along Penn Avenue cast dim shadows across the room. Her laptop sat on the island in the kitchen. She pulled out a stool, opened the lid, booted up the search engine, then typed *Ray Howell, Pittsburgh Daily Times*. Indeed, information on the newsman appeared. Except it was merely an archive site of the paper with a list of articles he'd written for the now-defunct publication. She scrolled through the list. No article was available on the collective murders of three women from Pittsburgh in 1953. Hm.

Moving on, she typed in *John Hermann, 1953*. Absolutely no information was listed on the man whatsoever. Alexa drew her fingers away from the keyboard. Well, how stupid would it be for the result of these murders to be so readily available? Too easy, and surely Pete knew that a mortal, such as herself, might be inclined to cheat. "Touché, Pete," she muttered under her breath. She typed in one more thing: *shoe shops and repair, Pittsburgh 1950s*. The *Pittsburgh Post-Gazette* had an old article that claimed when Joe's Shoe Repair opened their doors, they were one of 40,000 shops in the U.S., and now only 7,000 remain. *Wow*. With that, she closed the lid of the laptop.

She was wide awake and considering making her way downstairs to take in the fire damage in the kitchen. Alexa had been completely used up last night and decided to let it wait until morning. Hey, she'd handled enough for one day: investigating murders, driving Bobby's old wreck around the city, identifying a body, firing Stacia, and hiring Holden. Yep, it had seemed enough for one day. Then she noticed her cell phone lying on the other end of the island. Wow, she hadn't even thought about checking her messages. Perhaps 1953 was having a bigger influence on her than she realized. She slipped from the stool and made her way to the other end to pick up the phone. She had six missed calls—most from Nat. Five text messages, four from Nat, about the offer on the house, no doubt, and there was one from...Cliff! Her heart pounded inside her chest as she touched the message sent from the sexy police detective...

> *Hi, just wanted to let you know*
> *that I'm thinking about you and*
> *looking forward to Saturday.*

Dang! He'd sent that message almost twenty-four hours ago. She'd missed it, and she didn't want him to think she didn't care enough to answer. Thumbs racing across the keypad, she typed...

> *Hi! Just found this message.*
> *Crazy busy.*
> *Can't wait to see you!*

Alexa let out a relieved sigh. She hoped when he got the message, he would feel good about it. She couldn't let this Bobby Starr stuff get in the way of her earthly life, her earthly desires, and it was possible Pete was feeling the same way. She decided to go back to bed and try to get more sleep, with a wait-and-see attitude.

THE SUN GLARED THROUGH the bedroom window, directly into Alexa's eyes. No more did the cool breeze of night drift through the open window. The curtains stood still. It was instantly clear, and the morning of July 18th promised more heat and humidity for Pittsburgh. She rolled over to escape the sun's cruel morning rousing, only to find it was ten minutes after nine. Alexa shot up from the pillow. She'd forgotten to set an alarm. Why hadn't Winnie called or text-messaged her? She snatched her phone from the nightstand—two missed calls and one missed text message—all from Winnie. She must've been down for the count.

Alexa raced to the closet, rummaging through drawers and hangers to find something to wear. She chose a darling, short-sleeved, white peasant blouse and a pair of lightweight, navy blue and white striped loose slacks that featured a paper bag–tied waist. She dashed into the bathroom to wash, slap on some makeup, rake her hair into a ponytail, then stuffed a pair of rhinestone studs into her lobes. With no time left before the first customer was to arrive, she slipped into the same silver flip-flops she'd worn yesterday. One last check in the mirror—yes, acceptable. She'd grab a cup or five of coffee downstairs. She trotted out of her apartment and down the stairs. Almost to the bottom, she saw Holden walking past the stairs with a mug in hand. "Good morning," she called out just as the flip-flop on her right foot curled under her foot. Her ankle gave, making her fall forward.

Holden dropped the mug and lunged forward to catch her in his arms. They were nose to nose when she heard Cliff's voice. "So, I guess that's why you're so crazy busy."

Still locked in the embrace, Alexa and Holden turned in time to see Cliff spin on his heels and march out of the shop.

"Uh, oh," Holden began. "I'm guessing that's Cliff. Well, this certainly gives the wrong impression."

Alexa pushed away from the clinch to rush toward the door. "Cliff!" But her call was of little use. That downward suction started. Her head began to spin. She was headed for 1953 at the worst possible moment, and it was abruptly clear that Pete had little concern for her earthly life or desires.

Chapter Thirteen

Rock Solid Plan

"Alexa...Alexa, are you okay?"

Bobby was shaking her. She rolled her head toward his voice. A wave of dizziness hit. She realized it might not be the transition from her time to 1953; the dizziness and nausea might be from the lack of food. The last time she remembered having anything to eat was the Danish at the coffee shop with Cliff on...when was that? A week ago? A month ago? It seemed that long. No, it was Tuesday—wait, that was yesterday.

"What's the matter with her?" Brian asked. The Irish bartender was blurry but slowly coming into view.

"Um...she's had a rough night," Bobby said. Clearly the man was not exactly quick on the draw.

Alexa grabbed his arm. "I need something to eat. Like, *now*."

"You heard the lady, get her a burger or somethin', Brian."

"Comin' right up! Molly! Get this lass a burger. First one off the grill!"

Alexa heard the sound of light, quickened feet heading for the kitchen area. Finally Bobby had come into clear view. He asked, "Are you gonna be okay? This is the worst you've been when you've returned."

Her voice came out on the shady side of terse. "I'm *not* okay. You and *Saint* Pete are killing my love life here."

The right side of Bobby's mouth hitched upward. "Ooh, the guy from your apartment the other night. What's his name?"

"Cl—you *really* don't want to know. Not to mention, I haven't had anything to eat since yesterday morning. We really need to stop for dinners while we're working. I'm a mortal, remember."

"Ah, yes, we must feed the mortals," Bobby said around a snort.

"Cute. Very cute." She shifted on the stool. Just then, her black purse slipped from her lap to the floor with a hefty *thunk*. Alexa flinched. She hadn't noticed the purse on her lap.

Bobby scooped the purse up and handed it to her. "Whoa, what have you got in that thing? It's really heavy."

Quickly, Alexa unsnapped the purse to peer inside. Yep, the Colt was still lying on the bottom next to the change purse and several personal items Pete evidently thought she would need, like a comb, hairpins and a lipstick case. "Um...I always keep a rock in my purse. You know, in case I have to protect myself."

Bobby slapped a folded-up newspaper onto the bar. "Looks like Howell got his scoop, without our help."

"Whoa, that's a newspaper, an actual, bona fide

newspaper," Alexa said, running her fingers over the front page.

Bobby blinked back. "You don't have newspapers in your time?"

"Yes...and no." She unfolded the paper to look at the front-page headline:

MURDERS OF THREE LOCAL WOMEN SOLVED
~ Ray Howell

Alexa rolled her eyes. "That's nice. They've tried and convicted John Hermann before they've got all the facts or the evidence. Seems nothing has changed in the last sixty years or so."

"Go ahead, read it. I've gotta admit, it's a convincing piece. But it can't be right, because I'm still here, and so are you," Bobby put in.

Alexa read the article out loud. "'Thanks to the quick work of this reporter and a reliable source, the man responsible for the murders of three local women is now behind bars. John Hermann, a local handyman, was arrested for the strangulation death of Louise Kinsley. The police are investigating his involvement in the murders of Cora Lee Starr and Marion Hill, the most recent victim. All three women were strangled and had a ring stolen from their bodies.

"'This reporter was approached last week by a man who said Hermann was doing repairs at a local shop, and he witnessed Hermann pick a ring out of his toolbox, look at it, then replace it in said toolbox. After finding Marion Hill's body in her home, it was quickly discovered by a friend that she too was missing a ruby ring. This reporter immediately informed the police of Hermann's actions, as per my source.

"'Upon searching Hermann's home, police found John Hermann in possession of the ring that once belonged to Louise Kinsley. He was arrested and charged with her murder, which took place in May. However, the police have not found any of the other victim's rings as of yet. An investigation is ongoing at this time.'" Alexa tossed the paper aside and turned to Bobby. "So, you've been working the case since I've been gone?"

A shrug. "Sort of."

"*Sort of*? That is *not* a good answer to that question, Bobby. That's the answer to a question like…hey, is that nasty rash you've got clearing up? *Sort of.*" She could feel a warm flush rising on her cheeks, and it wasn't the hunger. What little patience she had left for Bobby Starr was declining rapidly.

Bobby blinked back. Evidently he wasn't accustomed to women talking to him in such a manner. "Calm down. Of course I've been working the case. I'm not a *quitter*, ya know."

Alexa leaned her elbows on the bar. "Good, I'm all ears. What've ya got, Detective?"

Molly approached carrying a plate with a huge bun enveloping a juicy-looking burger. On the side was a tomato and a big slice of onion. She set the plate in front of Alexa, then reached into the pocket of her blue apron to retrieve a bottle of Heinz ketchup, which she sat down next to the plate. She smiled at Alexa, then her gaze slid to Bobby. "Are ya puttin' this on your *tab* too?"

"How much do I have so far?" Bobby asked.

"Including the burger, it's an even two dollars."

"I'll pay at the end of the week. Thanks, Mrs. Mulaney."

She tossed him a doubtful look, then walked away mumbling something under her breath. Alexa leaned in close to Bobby. "We'll be done here by the end of the week."

"Don't worry, the me from 1953 will pay the tab."

Slapping the onion onto the burger, Alexa shot him a baleful look. "How in God's name did *you* get into heaven?"

He grinned. "Like Howell says in the article, they're holding John Hermann, and I'm pretty sure he's gonna be charged with at least Louise's murder. He's denying he killed anyone—don't they all. John claims he has no idea how Louise's birthstone ring ended up in his toolbox."

"I'd like to know who Ray Howell's source is." Alexa took a big bite of the burger.

"So, you don't think Hermann is our guy?"

"I don't know," she managed around a mouthful. She chewed a bit more, then said, "It does bother me that Marion saw him arguing with Louise at the Stanley, right before she was killed. If we only knew what they were arguing about. There's really no way of finding out—Marion and Louise, the only two people who could have any idea, are both gone."

"I have to wonder if John told Mrs. Kinsley about the argument," Bobby put in. "It seemed to me he did a lot of work at her house. They must've talked about *something*, and Louise's death had to have come up at some point."

"That's very good. We should stop in and talk with her again. Anything else?" Alexa took another big bite. The burger was delicious. She could almost feel her arteries clogging up solid.

"I checked out the nail you found at Marion's house."

Whoa, the man was inspired. Maybe he did need to work solo for a while. Pete knew what he was doing.

"Turns out, lots of the shoemakers and shoe repair shops around town use them, Joe's on Fourth, Pete's, P&G's on Fifth, and they were all more than happy to educate me on their tools of the trade. But this little nail right here..." Bobby dug the nail out of his shirt pocket to hold it up between his thumb and forefinger. "It's silver. Most are brass or gold-colored. The shoemakers in the area told me the silver nails are expensive, so they use the other kinds. I've seen these at Baker's. Frank used them on the more expensive shoes he made, you know, for the wealthier customers."

"We'll check that out for sure. But let's visit with Mrs. Kinsley first. I'm really hoping she's had a conversation with John that will help. Is your car available?" she asked just before taking another bite.

Bobby hitched his chin up toward the window. Alexa turned, and there the old clunker sat, in all its rusted-out glory. "Yeah, I'm upstairs in the apartment, right now, with Catherine."

Holding her hands up in a halting manner, Alexa rolled her eyes. "Too much information. Let's just go." Slipping the purse over her arm, she jumped down from the stool, took up what was left of the burger, and headed for the door.

"I can't believe John would hurt Louise or Marion. He seemed like such a nice young man," Mrs. Kinsley explained as she handed Alexa and Bobby each a cup of tea from a small plastic tray.

It was so cold outside. Alexa wrapped her hands around the cup to warm them. She asked, "Since Louise's death, has John talked to you about that night?"

Mrs. Kinsley set the tray onto the coffee table, picked up her cup, then sank into her rocker. "No, not really."

"Marion told us that he spoke to Louise at the Stanley that evening. Did he mention that?"

She rocked back and forth several times, staring into her teacup. "Yes, he said he'd had words with Louise after the show. John felt so bad about it because it was the last time he spoke to her."

Bobby asked, "Did he say what they argued about?"

The rockers creaked against the wood floor. Resting her head back, Mrs. Kinsley closed her eyes. Alexa could see she was trying to decide what she wanted to reveal about her conversation with John Hermann. Bobby's expression reflected the questions running through Alexa's mind: Is she going to tell us or is she going to keep this to herself? And if so, why?

After a long rumination, Mrs. Kinsley dragged her eyes open. "John said that Louise was seeing a man. She hadn't been seeing him for very long, but John was trying to warn her about him. He said the man was very nice to women at first, then he would become demanding and rough. John didn't want to see her get hurt. But

I guess Louise wouldn't listen to him. I wish she had. I don't know if this man had anything to do with Louise's death, but I still wish she'd listened to John."

"Did John say who this man was?" Bobby asked.

"No, he wouldn't. He said he was keeping an eye on him, but he did say the man works in the Strip, and John does a lot of work in that section of town."

"Just one more thing, Mrs. Kinsley," Alexa said. "Do you happen to know if Marion bought shoes or had shoes made at a particular shoe shop?"

"I don't know. But she did come along with us to Baker's a time or two, when Louise and I were shopping. I went to school with Anna Baker. She was Anna Collins back then. We were friends, so I liked to do business with old friends. She did some hemming on several dresses for me and one for Louise too. I remember Marion loved a pair of shoes that were in the window, but they were too dear."

"Did you go to Baker's often?" Alexa inquired.

"I wouldn't say often. Maybe once or twice a year at the most. Mainly to have shoes repaired. Frank's shoes were very expensive, but his shoe repair service was affordable. We'd always have tea with Anna in the back room when we stopped in."

Alexa exchanged glances with Bobby. She fished. "When was the last time you stopped by Baker's Shoes?"

"Oh, my, I'd have to think about that." She brought her right hand to her lips and gazed down at the floor. It was obvious she was searching her mind for that visit to the shoe shop. She rocked back and forth, then the rocker stopped and her gaze lifted to meet Alexa's. "It was about two weeks before Louise's death. I remember, because Anna had decorated the window for Memorial Day with red, white, and blue bows. She'd placed shoes of the same colors in the window on stands. It was all done up for the holiday. It looked so pretty. Louise especially liked the red heels in the window, but they were so dear. The nice man who worked for Frank, he talks with an English accent, anyway, he suggested Frank discount the shoes for Louise, but Frank wasn't too keen on the idea." She chuckled at the memory.

Alexa pushed up from her seat and set her cup of tea on the tray. She grabbed up her purse. "Thanks so much for talking with us, Mrs. Kinsley."

"I hope I've been helpful," she said, easing onto her feet.

"Very. You take care," Alexa said. She followed Mrs. Kinsley to the door, with Bobby close behind.

Once they were off Mrs. Kinsley's front porch, Bobby had to almost jog to keep up with Alexa. "Where ya goin' in such a hurry?"

"We've got evidence to collect, and I've got a plan how to do just that," she announced over her shoulder. She almost giggled at the shock on Bobby's face when she jumped into the driver's seat of the old Chevy. He didn't object. He simply slid into the passenger's seat and tossed her the key. She twisted the key in the ignition. The car protested and grunted but finally stuttered to life. Alexa pressed down on the clutch, then shuffled the gear shift around until the clunker was moving in a forward direction.

"I think I'm on the same track as you are, but just to

be sure, what evidence are you talking about, and what does this plan involve?" Bobby asked.

Alexa grinned. "You sure do know the right questions to ask, Starr." He shot her a baleful look. "We need to find out who has possession of Cora and Marion's rings. My plan involves you, me, and there's a very good possibility it may require my rock."

Bobby glanced down at the purse lying on the seat next to her. His brows rose.

165

Chapter Fourteen

Risky Business

Bobby slid into a chair next to Alexa. He handed her a flashlight he'd just retrieved from his apartment. She dropped it into her purse. He glanced over his shoulder toward the bar where Martin Fitch had just ordered up a beer and was in the process of lighting a cigarette. The Lazy Hound was starting to come alive with regular patrons who stop in for a pint or two after work. "I dunno, Alexa. The more I think about it, the more it all sounds very risky."

"You're right, it is," Alexa said. "Want to know what's even riskier? Not solving Cora Lee's murder by midnight *tonight*. And…" She checked the clock that hung over the opening for the dumbwaiter behind the bar. "It's now almost four o'clock. We've *got* to do something to crack these cases wide open, and it's going to be risky, no matter what."

"Have you ever broken into a shop before?"

"No. And I wouldn't have to tonight if you still had

Cora Lee's key. Still, it's not like I'm breaking in to steal stuff. I mean, other than what we require…for evidence."

"What makes you so sure you're gonna find the evidence at the shop?"

"I'm not *sure*. I'm hopeful. If I don't find what I'm looking for, we'll have to look elsewhere, and that will involve tons more risk. That said, I'm going to need something different to wear. Something dark," Alexa explained. Instantly, her clothes transformed from the simple skirt and blouse she was sporting to a pair of black leggings, a black mock turtleneck sweater, and a black box jacket to keep her warm. The leggings weren't quite as tight as those worn in Alexa's time. They were a good bit looser, but they worked nonetheless. She was also pleased with the furry slip-on ankle boots. Alexa grinned at Bobby. "Well, look at this. Pete knew exactly what I needed. I'm feeling rather…blessed." She giggled to herself at the flash of panic in Bobby's eyes. He glanced around the pub. Luckily, no one seemed to be paying any attention to Alexa's sudden wardrobe change.

Bobby groused, "Yeah, well, don't get too cocky. Blessings can turn into troubles in a snap."

Alexa hitched her chin toward the bar. Martin was lifting a cold one to his lips. "Just keep an eye on Mr. Fitch. Don't let him leave the bar. Hopefully, I won't be too long."

She turned to leave. Bobby grabbed her arm. "I should come with you. *I'm* supposed to solve this murder, not you, Alexa."

She was proud of him. But she was smaller, stealthier. "If *our* suspicions are correct, you did solve it, Bobby. I'm just going to get what we need to wrap it up in a pretty package for the police."

"And if we're wrong?"

"Then it's back to figuring it all out with very little time left to do so."

"Be careful."

"Don't worry. I've got a gu...er...a rock with me." Before he could object any further, she wiggled her arm free and scooted out the door.

Retrieving a pack of cigarettes from his jacket, Bobby flopped down in a chair at a nearby table.

BOBBY SAID BAKER'S SHOE SHOP was not more than a half-block or so up the Strip on the other side of Penn Avenue. Alexa trotted across the street. The wind had picked up, and she could see a heavy flurry falling in the cast of light from the street lamps. Some of the shop windows were done up for the Christmas holiday. Jamming her hands into the pockets of her jacket, she hurried up the sidewalk. She wasn't sure how she was going to manage breaking into the shoe shop. Bobby had directed her to go down the alley between Baker's and a Hank's Sandwich Shop. He said there would be a back door that led into Anna's small workroom and a tiny kitchen. He assured her the lock on the door was rather flimsy and should be easily manipulated—with what, she wasn't quite sure. He warned her to stay clear of the front window once she was in the showroom, where the shoes were displayed, and the shoemakers worked. He said the street lamps illuminated the room well, and the police who walked that beat peered into the windows every time they passed.

Alexa's cheeks felt like ice cubes when the sandwich shop and Baker's Shoes came into view. She paused for several moments to admire the lovely selection of holiday footwear displayed in the window. A pair of red high heels with a glittery red bow draped over the pointed toes caught her attention immediately. They would look fab with some of her holiday attire she wore in the twenty-first century. She wondered how much they were, and what Mrs. Kinsley considered too dear or expensive. After all, a beer was a mere sixty-five cents in comparison to today's price of six to eight dollars. So, was an expensive pair of shoes five dollars, ten?

Before making her way down the dimly lit alley, Alexa looked up the street and down. Not too many people were out and about. Traffic along Penn was extremely light. Well, it was a cold and blustery Wednesday night. Everyone was probably at home with their families, eating dinner, doing homework, watching TV, or maybe listening to the radio—like all the elderly people say it used to be.

With no one to notice a dark figure creeping about, Alexa approached the apex of the alley. She swallowed hard. The alley was dark, and yes, scary. Several trash cans were stationed along the tall block walls with only a sliver of night sky between the rooftops of the two build-ings. She wasn't sure if the narrow road was even wide enough for a car to drive through. She was nervous about entering the shadowy throughway. Anyone or anything could be hiding among the shadows. Hold on. No need to fuss. She opened the purse and pulled out the Colt. Now she could travel through the passageway with confidence, while keeping alert for icy patches.

Finally, through the alleyway, Alexa approached three cement steps flanked with a rusty railing that led to a small stoop just outside the back door to Baker's Shoes. An old single-bulb lamp cast dim shadows over the weatherbeaten wood door. Alexa stuffed the gun into her jacket pocket and climbed the stairs furtively. She grabbed the doorknob and gave it a shake. It didn't budge. She had to smile. The lock was an old-fashioned keyhole-style lock, and she had a sudden idea of how to break in. She opened her purse and pulled out the package of hairpins, pulled one out, and bent it until it was straight. She looked over her shoulder to make sure the cop who walked this beat wasn't observing her from a distance. Satisfied that no one was watching, she pressed the hairpin into the keyhole and jiggled it around until she found the latch. Holding her breath, she pressed the hairpin and the latch clicked. Success! Alexa eased the door open and stepped into the small workroom. A Singer sewing machine was off to the right. Just beyond the sewing machine several dresses hung on a rack. The wall straight ahead held a huge, wooden shelving unit with all kinds of cobbler's supplies, shoe forms, leather, leather straps, hammers of different sizes and shapes, and more. The kitchenette was to the left, and ahead, next to the shelves, a dark blue curtain hung in a doorway. Alexa figured it led to the showroom. She didn't want to lug the purse with her. So, with the gun in her jacket pocket, she set the purse on the table. Okay, no time like the present. It was time to do what she'd come to do.

BOBBY SMASHED YET ANOTHER CIGARETTE into the ashtray as Maggie set yet another beer on the table before him. She gathered up his empty mug and moved on to the next table. His tab was rising. He was probably up to five, maybe six bucks by now. He hoped his 1953 counterpart was having a good month in the investigation biz, although he couldn't for the death of him remember what December of '53 had been like. He remembered being miserable, but he couldn't remember his case load or the lack thereof.

"Hey!" a man shouted from the door. Uh oh, Bobby recognized the voice—it was his own. He didn't dare turn to see what the problem could be. Instead, he grabbed up his fedora from the chair next to him, plopped it on his head, and pulled the brim down low. His former self yelled across the room, "Someone stole my Colt from my car! Has anyone seen anyone around my car?"

Bobby glanced up from under his hat to see Maggie's horrified expression. Her mouth was moving but nothing was coming out, and he knew what the problem was. Maggie was seeing double. She'd been serving up beer to Bobby Starr at the table, and yet, there he stood at the door frantic for answers about his stolen gun. Furthermore, Bobby was pretty sure he knew who had taken the gun, or the *rock,* as it were. No matter, it was time for him to make a quick exit. Bobby pushed up from his chair to stealthily slide along the wall until he reached the back exit of the bar—the entrance into the storeroom. Keeping his back to the pub, he pressed through the door.

Molly Mulaney was lifting a box marked Beer Nuts from a shelving unit when she turned to find him lingering near the door.

She lugged the box toward him. "Honest to St. Patrick himself. I've never had anyone scoot out the back door as much as you do, Mr. Starr." Molly wasn't making a casual observation. Rather, her voice dripped with reprimand.

"I'll try to curb the habit," Bobby said.

"See that you do, then," Molly stated over her shoulder, as she pushed through the door into the pub.

Bobby grabbed the door to hold it open just a bit so he could peek into the pub. Bobby from 1953 was traveling from person to person, asking if they knew anything about the missing gun. People shook their head no, and Maggie continued to stare rather than wait her tables. Finally, frustrated with no information, 1953 Bobby stomped up the stairs.

Bobby let out a relieved breath. He'd dodged that bullet. Except, that's when he noticed Martin's empty stool. He stepped halfway through the door, scanning the pub—Martin was gone. Brian was gathering up Martin's mug from the bar and wiping up the spot. Molly set down the box of nuts, then made her way along the back of the bar.

Bobby darted across the room, passing a still stunned Maggie. "Where did Martin go?"

"He left a moment ago," Brian replied over his shoulder, as he poured a pint from the tap.

"And he left through the *front* door," Molly put in, as she lifted a tub of dirty mugs from under the bar.

"Did he say where he was goin'?" Bobby asked. He could feel a surge of panic racing through him.

Brian pushed the pint down the bar toward a man four stools away. "He'd forgotten his wallet at the shop. He went to get it. Hope he comes back soon. I don't really trust him that much."

Bobby pushed away from the bar to dart out the front door.

Chapter Fifteen

Stilettos are a Girl's Best Friend

After pressing through the blue curtain that separated the workroom from the showroom, Alexa stood very still, considering the space before her. Bobby was right. The street lamps did a fine job of brightening the room. She was having no trouble seeing everything; still, she was glad to have the little flashlight Bobby had retrieved from his old apartment. A round display table draped in holiday fabric held as many as ten pairs of shoes—men's, women's, and a few children's shoes as well. Taking up the entire length of wall to the right were floor-to-ceiling shelves filled with all kinds of shoes. Straight ahead was the storefront window, and to its left, the door. To the far right of the room were two shoemaker's workbenches, just as Bobby had described.

She thought placing the workbenches in the showroom where the customers perused products, rather than in the back room with Anna, was odd. But Bobby explained that Frank, Cora Lee's father, liked being among the patrons to answer any questions they might have about the shoes or the construction of the shoes. Old-fashioned pride in one's craft. Supposedly, the bench to the right belonged to Frank and the one to the left, Martin.

Alexa took a step toward the benches, then quickly ducked behind the circular display table when she heard someone whistling a tune from outside. She peeked from behind the tablecloth to watch a police officer peer into the storefront window and then continue down the sidewalk, returning to his tune as he went. When the sound of his song seemed farther down Penn, Alexa emerged from her hiding place to creep across the shop toward the benches closely lined up side by side against the wall. She was amazed. She'd expected much larger cobbler's benches. Both wooden benches were affixed to the wall. Shoe forms of all shapes and sizes were lined up along the very top of the cabinets. The cabinets featured a dozen drawers, six in each row of two, across the top, and two large shelves and two smaller, narrower shelves below. A thick wooden counter jutted out from the cabinet with an attached chair. The chair had a scoop in the seat that looked like it was fitted for one's bottom. Beneath the counter were two larger drawers. Frank's bench was tidy and unused. On the other hand, Martin's bench had an active production look to it. Leather hung from the lower large drawers. But it was what was on the counter that snagged Alexa's immediate attention—a pair of stiletto heels. Scattered around the shoes were nails, a knife, two spools of thread, and remnants of leather, along with an ashtray overflowing with cigarette butts.

She took two measured steps toward the benches, stopped to check the window, then continued until she reached Martin's workplace. The shoes were made of... hold the phone...was that actual *alligator* skin? She ran her fingers over the toe of one of the shoes, feeling the softened scales, then gasped. Indeed, they were the real McCoy—alligator skin stilettos! Gorgeous! The shoes had to be a special order. Those sexy babies would be worth at least four, no, *five* hundred dollars in the twenty-first century. Alexa had to wonder how much they would go for in 1953, and who had ordered them.

As much as she would have loved to try them on, there was no time for such nonsense. Alexa eyed up the brass knobs on the drawers and decided it was as good a place to start as any. Starting at the top left, she pulled the first drawer open. It was long and narrow; it just seemed to keep coming and coming until she'd pulled it all the way out. She laid it on the counter to examine the contents. The drawer was filled with accessories to bling up women's shoes: ribbon, rhinestone buttons, and so on. She turned the contents of the drawer over in her fingers, looking for jewelry among the bling. Nothing. Eleven more drawers to go.

By the time Alexa had opened the twelfth drawer, she was frustrated with finding nothing but cobbler's tools and supplies. She rifled through the shelves—the two large shelves and then the smaller ones. No rings. Drawing back from the bench, she let out a beleaguered sigh. Okay, maybe she was wrong. Maybe the shoemaker's nail had nothing to do with Marion's death. Like Bobby had suggested, maybe it simply fell out of a shoe. Her eyes slid toward Frank's quiet, abandoned bench. Hm, if she were using a workbench on a daily basis, would she hide something in it or would she place small, stolen items in a bench that no one paid any mind to?

Crossing her arm over her chest, she leaned against Martin's bench to scrutinize Frank's, and that's when she noticed a tiny drawer in the lower portion of the bench, toward the back, snug to the wall. The benches had been stationed so tightly together, with little more than a foot between. She could understand why no one would notice the cubby, unless one was studying the benches closely, as she was. She pulled the flashlight from her left pocket and shined its light on the cubby. The drawer appeared to be a late addition to the bench. Interesting. What would Frank Baker need to hide? She leaned forward to see if Martin had such a drawer—none on this side. She rushed around the bench to look on the other side—no drawer. Checking the window again, she made her way toward Frank's bench, squeezed between the two, then squirmed and wiggled to get down on her knees between the benches. Not much room to work. She stuck the flashlight in her mouth and shined it toward the drawer.

There was no handle on the drawer, just a little carved notch scarcely big enough to slide one's finger inside and tug. The cubby was definitely used as a hiding place. She maneuvered her finger around until she could slip it into the notch, then she pulled on the covert drawer, but it wouldn't budge. Alexa examined it more closely. There was no lock. Maybe it hadn't been opened in quite some time and was just stuck. She pulled again and again, until finally, the drawer slide partially open, and just enough for her to slip four fingers inside. She felt around and came up with a small, round tin. She spent some time jiggling the tin, then managed to pull it up through the gap sideways. She felt something else in the cubby, something long. It felt leathery. *Never mind that for now.* Alexa sat back on the floor, removed the flashlight from her mouth to examine the round container in her hands. The little box once held chewing tobacco, Skoal. Hm, maybe Frank didn't want Anna to know he chewed tobacco while making shoes. Then again, what was the difference? Everybody smoked back in the day. Obviously, Martin smoked while at his bench, with the dirty, stinky ashtray on the counter directly next to the fabulous alligator shoes. Like the pub, the showroom had a lingering smell of stale cigarette smoke.

She shook the tin, and something rattled inside. More than one something. It sounded like several somethings. Carefully, she twisted the top. Shining the light on the tin, her breath caught. Lying in the bottom of the tin were a wedding band, a ruby ring, and two diamond rings.

"My God, he's killed more than three women," Alexa muttered.

"Whatcha got there, bint?"

Alexa's eyes snapped upward to find Martin Fitch standing over her. Her heart skipped five beats. The flashlight slipped from her hand. Her throat was instantly dry. Quickly, she clamped the lid onto the tin, and shoved it into her pocket, grabbing hold of the gun. Except she was not only trapped but wedged so tightly that once she got her hand into the pocket, she couldn't get it back out. In the distance, she could hear someone whistling a tune.

Martin's face held a dangerous edge. There was no question in Alexa's mind his intentions were wicked. The gun was in her grip in her right pocket. Her left hand was free. Good thing Martin's bench was to her left. She eyed the stilettos—when she'd taken self-defense classes, the instructors always pointed out that *anything* can be used as a weapon. Sometimes one had to be creative, and this was one of those times. In the next heartbeat, Martin grabbed the front of her jacket to haul her to her feet and out of the snug space.

"Think you're gonna get away with me treasures then, bint?" Martin growled.

As he yanked her forward, Alexa grabbed up one of the stilettos and slammed the long, pointed heel into his right eye. Crying out in pain, Martin jerked backward, letting go of her and pitching the shoe toward the front window, knocking down a good bit of the holiday display. Scowling in agony, he grabbed his eye. Askance, she saw a shadow pass by the window, but she couldn't take her attention away from Martin. She pulled the gun from her pocket to point it directly at him. He lunged forward, and the opportunity of a lifetime showed itself. As she kept the gun steady and trained on Martin, she said, "Go ahead! Make my day, Fitch!" It was the greatest line ever spoken in a movie, well, in Alexa's opinion anyway. It was a line exclusive to the great Clint Eastwood, but at this moment, Alexa Owl owned it, and Martin reacted—he froze in his place.

Keeping his hand over his eye, Martin said, "You ain't got what it takes to shoot the likes of me."

Alexa's lips curled. "Well, you've got to ask yourself,

do I feel *lucky*?" She cocked the gun. God, Clint would be so proud of her. Martin eased back.

"So, *that's* who took my *rock*. Somehow, I'm just not surprised," Bobby said.

Alexa chanced a glance to find Bobby standing just beyond the blue curtain. "It was right there for the taking. We need to have a serious discussion about gun safety, Detective Starr." She pulled the tin from her pocket and tossed it to him. "I found this in a secret cubby in Frank's workbench. We need to take another look. There's something else in there that I couldn't get out."

Bobby twisted the lid open. "Cora's wedding band," he whispered. Alexa could hear the pain in his voice. He held up the ruby ring. "Is this what I think it is?"

"Marion's pigeon blood ruby, yes," Alexa said.

"But there's..."

"That's right. There're two diamond rings in there. I think you know what that means."

"You found that stuff in Frank's bench, not mine. I ain't never seen those rings before," Martin griped.

"Cut the crap, Fitch. You're Ray Howell's source, and you know all about the rings, and more," Alexa said.

"Put the gun down, Miss Owl," Detective Slater's voice rang out from across the room. Alexa's attention whipped toward the familiar voice to find the detective, flanked by two police officers, guns trained on them, standing just inside the blue curtain.

"That bint was robbin' the bloody shop. She assaulted me," Martin cried out, pointing an accusing finger with his right hand, while moving his left to reveal his bruised and bleeding eye.

"I don't know what a *bint* is, but you can *stop* calling me that," Alexa demanded, as she dropped the Colt to the floor. She was shocked to find the tin in her hand, and she instantly held it up for Slater to see. "I wasn't robbing the shop. That said, I did find the murdered women's missing rings, plus *two* more." She turned, looking for confirmation from Bobby. He was gone. He'd disappeared into thin air. How convenient. She was well aware he could vanish in her time, but why hadn't he mentioned his ability to do such a thing in 1953? What a pain-in-the-butt ghost!

"We'll get this all sorted out down at the station. Get them in the cars, boys. I'll do my best to secure the back door for Mrs. Baker," Slater instructed.

"Wait!" Alexa insisted. "I found this tin filled with Cora Lee Starr's wedding band, Marion Hill's pigeon blood ruby, and two more rings." She handed the box to Slater. He screwed it open, then his hard gaze cut to Martin. Alexa added, "I found it in that tiny drawer on the back side of Frank Baker's workbench. Thing is, there's something else in the drawer that I couldn't get a hold of. Please, just take a moment to look."

Slater studied Alexa for a moment. "Where? Show me."

Quickly, Alexa turned toward the benches and pointed. "Frank's bench is the one on the right. See there in the back? The drawer is still open just a bit. It's stuck. That's why I couldn't get the other item out."

Slater hitched his chin for the officers to pull one of the benches from the wall. Martin spoke up, "Here now! Those are attached to the wall. I don't know where that box came from. I had nothing to do with this, nothing I say!"

"We don't want to do any more damage to Mrs. Baker's shop. Miss Owl, can you squeeze back in there and try to get your hand inside the drawer?"

"I'd be glad to." Alexa shimmied in between the benches, picked up the flashlight, then squeezed down to her knees. Slater followed her to the edge of the bench, craning his neck to see what she was doing. "Here's the drawer. Hold the light, please." She handed Slater the light, then pulled and tugged. The drawer slid open a tiny way. She slipped the four fingers on her right hand into the gap. The object felt like leather. With two fingers she inched it closer to the front of the drawer.

"See here now! That's private property!" Martin challenged.

Finally, she managed to pull a bit of the object out of the drawer. Alexa's eyes widened. "Oh, my God, it's a strap!" She pulled it out to hold it in the air. "Looks like we've got the rings and the murder weapon, gentlemen."

Slater turned to an officer who was now standing next to Martin. "Cuff him, Tim." He took the strap from Alexa's hand. "It's a good thing we stopped by the Hound for a break, when we got the call that Tim saw someone in Bakers' shop. Although I don't think you would've been his next victim. It looked like you had things well in hand. That said, we have to take you down to the station, Miss Owl. You broke into this shop. But something tells me Mrs. Baker won't be pressing charges."

Chapter Sixteen

Who's Got Your Back?

Bobby leaned against the doorjamb of Ray Howell's office. The right side of his mouth hitched upward at the sight of the reporter completely immersed in the words he was pounding out on his typewriter. Alexa was right. Howell had his fingers in John Hermann's arrest. It wasn't a newsman's hunch, but rather a newsman's greed, and though he had nothing to do with the murders himself, he'd trusted the wrong man. He'd trusted a killer, and it was time to force the newsman to come clean. Bobby figured he might have to stretch the truth just a little, and Pete might not completely approve, but he believed Pete had an understanding how a P.I. worked. Bobby strolled toward Ray's desk, tossed the folded newspaper onto the man's lap, then he eased down into a chair.

Startled, Ray pulled his fingers away from the keys of the typewriter. His eyes flashed toward Bobby, then to the clock on the wall: seven o'clock. "How did you get in here?"

"I've got my ways." Resting his elbows on the arms of the chair, Bobby folded his hands across his stomach to announce, "This just in: Reporter Ray Howell's source on the murders of three local women has been arrested for those murders. All charges dropped against John Hermann. Yep, that sounds about right, because Fitch is telling Slater all about it as we speak."

Ray's entire body stiffened against his chair. He slapped the newspaper onto his desk, hard. "What are you talking about, Starr? Where's your latest flame, Miss Owl?"

Crossing his right leg over his left, Bobby removed his fedora and hung it on his knee. "She's down at the precinct helping Mr. Fitch, *your source*, unburden his soul. She's good at that sort of thing—brings out the best in people. I know she's had a great impact on me, that's for sure."

"Unburden himself about *what*? John Hermann is responsible for those girls' deaths. Fitch told me he *saw* Hermann with one of the rings when he was working at Baker's Shoes recently. He said he saw him look at the ring and put it back in his toolbox."

"Yeah, I read all about it in your article. Only, here's the thing—John Hermann is innocent. Fitch had possession of Cora's wedding band and Marion Hill's ruby, plus two more rings. They were found in one of the workbenches at the shop just a while ago. Something tells me he planted Louise Kinsley's ring in John's toolbox when he was doing repairs at the shop the other day." Bobby pointed at the newspaper lying on Ray's desk. "What a great scoop you had just yesterday. Too bad you'll be writing a retraction for tomorrow. Wonder how your editor's gonna feel about that." Bobby pushed up from the chair, plopped the fedora onto his head, then took a step toward the door.

"Wait a minute, Starr!" Ray jumped to his feet. "You're sure about this? You're *sure* Martin Fitch is the murderer and John Hermann is innocent?"

Bobby turned and grinned. "As sure as I'm standing here." With that, he vanished.

IT HAD BEEN A LONG, GRUELING EVENING at the police station. Alexa was charged with breaking and entering. It wasn't long until a shaken Anna Baker showed up. Detective Slater explained the circumstances, and all charges were dropped. Alexa felt the need to hang around until Martin Fitch was charged with the murders of Louise Kinsley, Cora Lee Starr, and Marion Hill. Even though she didn't know him, she wanted to see John Hermann walk out of the jail a free man.

Alexa had no idea where Bobby Starr had disappeared to. Maybe Pete had lifted him away, yet she still remained. Why? Nonetheless, it was almost nine o'clock, and Detective Slater was kind enough to have an officer drive her to the Lazy Hound. If Bobby Starr happened to be there, she was going to give him a piece of her mind. If he wasn't, she was going straight to panic mode. After all, she was still stuck in 1953, and that wasn't where she belonged.

The officer dropped her off just outside the Hound. The snow was falling hard and steady. Penn Avenue was covered with at least an inch. The hoods on the street lamps were coated. Alexa bid the officer goodbye, then waded through the snow-covered sidewalk to the door of the Hound. When she stepped inside, frustration instantly coiled through her. There he was, Detective Bobby Starr, sitting at the farthest end of the bar with young Winnie. Only several patrons sat at the bar, smoking and drinking. She couldn't believe he'd just abandon her at the shoe shop with the police glaring at her like she was a common criminal. He didn't back her up. She was left to her own devices. What a gutless ghost! Well, enough was enough. He was going to get a good tongue lashing and maybe a bit more! Alexa marched directly toward him.

"It's way past Winnie's bedtime, Mr. Starr. She'll have to finish her work in the mornin' before she's off to school," Molly insisted, as she removed her apron and flung it on the bar.

"Ah, c'mon, Mrs. Mulaney, there's just one more, and it's an easy one." He turned to Winnie. "Now, listen carefully. Sally and her family eat two loaves of bread a day. Each loaf provides six slices. How many slices of bread do Sally and her family eat in four days?"

"Thanks for having my back, *Detective* Bobby Starr!" Alexa grabbed the tall glass of beer sitting in front of him. He spun on his stool looking at her with a baffled expression, as she poured the beer over his head, and unfortunately onto the child's homework. Shocked, Molly took a step backward.

Jerking back, Bobby blew the foam from his face. Alexa spun on her heels to march out of the bar. She heard him yelling after her, "Hey! Come back here!" But

Alexa wasn't listening. She pushed through the door, hoping Pete would vacuum her back to the twenty-first century in the next nanosecond. That's when she came face to face with the ghostly Bobby Starr.

He smiled. "Wrong Bobby Starr, sweetheart."

Alexa balled her hands into tight fists at her sides. "UGH! Where've you been? You lousy, no-good-for—"

"Now, now, no need to resort to name-calling, Mrs. Owl. Pete wouldn't like you using bad language." Bobby glanced over his shoulder, then swiftly, he pushed her against the wall, imprisoning her between his arms, pressing his forehead to hers, yet she felt no weight of his head against hers. Bobby Starr from 1953 hurried past, got into the old wreck of a Chevy, and after several tries to bring it to life, he finally managed to drive into the snow-fallen night. When the Chevy had reached the red light, Bobby pulled back. "Sorry to leave you in the lurch like that, but I had to go. I didn't want Slater to see me. I mean, there are two of me, ya know. So, I decided to visit our favorite reporter, Ray Howell. You were right. Ray knew about the rings. Fitch had planted the ring on John Hermann, then told Ray about it. Pretty smart plan. He planted the ring in the toolbox of a man who worked for either the victim of the murders, or a family member, then he had a respected newspaper reporter send the police in Hermann's direction, diverting any attention from himself, that is, until he left a little piece of himself behind at Marion Hill's home. If you hadn't found that nail and run with your suspicions, we might still be trying to figure this out."

"Maybe. But I can't help but wonder who else he's murdered. There were two other rings in that tin, Bobby."

"I remember that Martin came to the shop shortly after I started seeing Cora. He may have killed those women in England. That's Slater's concern now. He's a good detective, he'll find out who those rings belong to. I know who killed my Cora, and that's what matters." Bobby's gaze dropped to the snowy sidewalk.

"You loved her."

He slowly dragged his gaze to meet Alexa's. "Yes, I truly did. And while I was with her, there was no other."

Alexa crossed her arms over her chest. "You really are like Henry the 8th."

Bobby blinked back. "Again, I *never* beheaded any of my wives."

Alexa giggled. "Of course, not. But when Henry the 8th was asked which of his six wives he loved the most he said Jane Seymour. He said he truly loved her."

"But he beheaded her anyway?"

"*No.* Jane Seymour died soon after childbirth. Hey, here's a thought. You were supposed to solve Cora Lee's murder, but you ended up solving *three* murders—Cora Lee's, Louise's, and Marion's. I wonder if Pete will give you credit for the three murders you need to solve to get into the squad."

Bobby tossed her a baleful look. "It's not like extra credit book reports, Alexa. Besides, I had to solve three murders *I* left behind."

Alexa lifted a shoulder and let it drop. "Doesn't hurt to ask."

He shot her a doubtful look. "Something tells me Pete's gonna stick to the original requirements."

"It's well after nine o'clock. I wish we could've

wrapped this up earlier—cutting it too close for my comfort level," Alexa put in.

"Time to spare, sweetheart. Time to spare."

"You're way too cool for your own good, Starr."

He grinned that annoying, but oh, so handsome boyish grin, and then she felt herself being sucked down into the vacuum. She was leaving Bobby Starr behind and going home to the twenty-first century.

Chapter Seventeen

Back to the Future

Alexa's eyes fluttered open. The bedroom was draped in darkness. Only the slight light of the street lamps along the parking lot behind her building spilled through the curtains. She flinched at the sound of the air conditioning kicking on, prompting her to push up from the pillows. Gone was the dark clothing she garbed moments ago, or rather, sixty-eight years ago. Instead, she was wearing a comfy pair of pink and gray plaid pajama pants and a pink cami. A feeling of relief and peace filled her to her soul. Cora Lee's murder had been solved. She glanced at the chair next to the window, and much to her pleasure, there was Garbo curled up on the seat of the chair, sound asleep. No longer was she keeping vigil over her former mistress's murder scene—end of watch. Her figure was completely translucent. Alexa could see the cream tufted pads of the chair through Garbo's body. Her glittery collar with the silver name tag seemingly hung in midair.

A svelte smile lifted Alexa's lip. She whispered, "Sleep easy, sweet Garbo." With that, Alexa snuggled into the pillows and closed her eyes.

It seemed but only moments later when the alarm on Alexa's cell phone stirred her. Sunshine shone through the long windows, and for the first time in a week, she felt rested and ready to face her day. Tossing the blankets aside, she sat up. Immediately her eyes went to the chair near the window. Garbo was gone. Her glittery collar lay on the chair. She'd gone to be with her mistress, Cora Lee. Alexa giggled to herself. Another cat for Saint Pete to chase off the Lord's chair. She lifted from the mattress and took up the collar from the chair to lay it on her nightstand, then went into the bathroom to prepare for whatever today threw at her. A stab of regret pierced her heart. Most likely she wouldn't be hearing from Cliff Slater. Most likely that chance at romance had sailed out to sea, burned and sunk. She turned on the shower.

"THIS SUIT IS ABSOLUTELY PERFECT. Fits me like a glove, a very comfortable glove. You did a fantastic job, Alexa. Don't you think so, Miff?" Hayden Mann turned to his wife, who was sitting on the sofa in the middle of the shop with Tinkerbell tucked under her arm. Miffie nodded her approval.

"Thank you, Mr. Mann. I'm so glad you're pleased. I'll be sure to tell my tailor, Holden. He did a lot of the finish-up work on the suit. By the way, I wanted to ask you about someone," Alexa said. "Have you ever heard of a newsman by the name of Ray Howell?"

Hayden chuckled. "Almost every reporter in the city has heard of Ray Howell, my dear. When I was a young reporter, back in the early sixties, he was *the* example. Wait, how did it go? Oh, yes, *Howell* to lose your credibility in the newspaper industry. If I remember correctly, he used a source to point the finger at a local man for the murders of several young women in the area. I don't recall the entire circumstance, but it turned out that his source was actually the murderer. Well, I guess Howell tried to cover it up, and things just got worse. Turned out, his source..." He paused, sucking in his lips, shaking his head, obviously trying to recall something. "I can't remember the guy's name, but anyway, turned out he'd murdered several women in the London area... London, England, before coming to the U.S. The guy would keep their rings as a trophy. It was a bad situation at best."

"Sounds like it. Whatever happened to Ray Howell?" Alexa inquired.

Another chuckle. "He ended up writing a gardening column for a small newspaper in Akron, Ohio. Too bad, it was said that he was on the cutting edge of a big-time career. Moral of the story—*always* check your sources, then check them again. Did you know him?"

"No, I heard that very story the other day and just wondered if you knew him. I'm so glad you like your suit, Mr. Mann. I hope you'll recommend my services to others."

"Absolutely, my dear. Absolutely."

With his new suit in hand and ready for his daughter's upcoming wedding, Hayden Mann left the shop along with his wife, Miffie, and her Chihuahua, Tinkerbell. "Tinkie-Winkie was happier in that shop this time," Alexa heard Miffie say on their way out the door.

Of course she was. Garbo wasn't swatting and hissing at her, Alexa thought.

The shop was quiet. It was lunchtime and Winnie had gone up the street for a sandwich, while Holden was running a personal errand. Having the place to herself, she turned out the chandeliers, kicked off her shoes, eased down on the sofa, crossing her left ankle over her right on the ottoman to relax a bit before Winnie and Holden returned. The next round of customers was expected around one o'clock.

Bobby Starr drifted into her thoughts. Were he and Cora Lee reconciled in heaven? What would that look like? She had no idea. Leaning her head back, she closed her eyes. It felt good to be back in the twenty-first century. Good to be home in her new shop. Suddenly, the shop's buzzer rang out, alerting her to a walk-in customer. She opened her eyes to find Cliff walking toward her with a take-out coffee cup in each hand.

He smiled. "So, I'm sitting at my desk at the precinct and this guy walks up to me and says that you're one gorgeous woman. A little clumsy, but gorgeous. He said if he liked women, he'd be all about you, but he's got a partner, and I'd be a real *idiot* to let you get away."

Alexa pushed up to a sitting position. "Is that what he told you? He called me clumsy?"

"Yep, that's what Mr. Emery said. Well, I'm thinking he's right, about the gorgeous part anyway. I also thought roses are *way* too cliché for a woman like you, so I took a gamble and brought you a latte instead." He sat down on the other end of the sofa. "I'm sorry, Alexa. I was way off base. Will you give me another chance? Are we still on for Saturday night?"

She looked into those incredibly intense hazel eyes, and she knew where he'd gotten them from. His grandfather was an honorable man, and Cliff was too. Something told her that she'd be a real idiot to let him go.

Cliff interrupted her thoughts. "Let me go one better. Why don't I show up here with all the ingredients, and I'll make you one of my famous Chicago pizzas?"

"You cook too?"

Cliff chuckled. "Holden thought you'd be impressed."

Her heart swelled. Winnie was right. Holden was going to work out just fine. Alexa smiled. "You had me at latte."

ALEXA FLOPPED DOWN ON THE SOFA. The day's last customer had just walked out the door. Fiona Quinn still hadn't set a wedding date, but she had a fabulous gown on hand for whenever the wedding happened.

"Where's your cat?" Fiona had asked during the final fitting.

Alexa stilled. "Um, that wasn't my cat. I was watching Garbo for a friend."

"You're a very good friend, Alexa," Fiona replied and it struck Alexa that she wished she had been friends with Cora Lee.

Winnie locked the door behind Fiona, then made her way to the bar. "I see ya decided to accept the offer on your parents' house, then."

"Yes. The offer is in the manila envelope on the cash desk. She said she'd stop by tomorrow to pick it up. I'm feeling relieved. Nat will be happy to hear it's all done too," Alexa said.

Winnie approached the sofa with a glass of wine in each hand. "I've been saving this for ya all day. Thought you might like a little wine to celebrate your recent successes." Alexa took one of the glasses from Winnie's hand. "Are ya glad to be done with Bobby Starr and his conundrum?"

"Oh, yes. I'm glad for how it all turned out. And I hope to never lay eyes on that ghost again," Alexa stated.

Winnie sagged onto the sofa, then lifted her glass. "Here's to learnin' from the mistakes of others. After all, you can't possibly live long enough to make them all yourself."

They clinked glasses. Alexa took a sip of her wine, a lovely pinot noir. "Winnie, can I ask you something?"

"Why, certainly, lass. What is it?"

Alexa let out a careworn sigh. "I was there when your sister, Elenore, ran away to get married. Your father was so upset. Your mother was heartbroken…"

"Ah, and you're wonderin' what came of it all. Me father was a strict Catholic, you know, and an even more stubborn man. He never forgave Ellie. We weren't allowed to contact her. Me father died on his seventieth birthday. I took care of me parents, but I wrote to Ellie all the time, and after me father's death, I told me mother that Ellie had three darlin' children. I told her she'd be a fool to go to her grave without laying eyes upon them or huggin' them to her chest." Winnie took a long drink of the wine.

"Did she go?" Alexa asked. Her heart was in her throat. She so wanted to know there was forgiveness between mother and daughter, and a family healed after so many years of separation over such a silly cause.

"She didn't even have to think about it. We were packed and on our way to New Jersey the very next mornin'. I've never seen two people hug as long as me mother and Ellie did. But I couldn't help but think of all the wasted years. All the years me parents could have been lovin' those grandchildren. At least me mother knew them for five years before her passing."

Alexa sank deeper into the sofa. "I wish Brian had too. I wanted so badly to tell them what a mistake they were making, and that in the future it didn't matter what religion or color two people were, as long as there was love and respect. But I couldn't, of course. Saint Pete was quite clear about the rules. Bobby and I were not permitted to do anything to change events. And we stuck to the protocol as closely as possible."

"So, other than solving Cora Lee's murder and sending the right man to jail, you don't think you changed any other events?"

Alexa took a sip of her wine. "If we did, we were totally unaware."

Epilogue

Behind the shield of the snow-covered rhododendron along the walk toward the old McCook mansion on Fifth Avenue, he waited for the lovely blonde, Shirley. After the McCook mansion had been sold to the Bonavita family in 1949, they rented the upper rooms to Carnegie Tech students to help in the upkeep of the old house. Tightening the leather strap around his fists, Martin waited. Then heard her hurried footfalls approaching.

Shirley pulled her coat tighter around her shoulders. The evening air was frigid, and she was a bit later than usual coming home from rehearsals at the Playhouse. No matter, he'd bided his time. He'd been patient. She didn't have much farther to walk to reach the mansion. She was about fifteen feet away. She was humming a tune, probably something she'd just rehearsed. Ten feet away. He could see the soft glow of moonlight glistening on her lovely face. She rushed past. Now! Now was the time to attack, to wrap the strap around her throat.

He leapt from his hiding place, fingers spread wide, reaching for her hair...his fingers raked through her long blonde tresses as he disintegrated into the night air.

Shirley hesitated, glancing over her shoulder, and then continued down the path and into the mansion.

THE END

About C.S. McDonald

For twenty-six years C.S. McDonald's life whirled around a song and a dance. Classically trained at Pittsburgh Ballet Theater School, The Pittsburgh Dance Alloy, and many others, she became a professional dancer and choreographer. During that time, she choreographed many musicals and an opera for the Pittsburgh Savoyards. In 2011 she retired from her dance career to write. Under her real name, Cindy McDonald, she writes murder-suspense and romantic suspense novels. In 2014 she added the pen name C.S. McDonald to write children's books for her grandchildren. In 2016 she added the Fiona Quinn Mysteries to that expansion. She decided to write the cozy mystery series that everyone, including teens and tweens, can read and enjoy. Presently, the Fiona Quinn Mysteries include nine books, with a tenth slated for 2021. The books are also available on audio, narrated by Maren Swenson Waxenberg.

Cindy's newest venture is The Owl's Nest Mysteries. Once again, she has set her cozy mystery in Pittsburgh and the female protagonist, Alexa Owl, is much different from Fiona Quinn. The Owl's Next Mysteries has a little grit, a little time travel, a little romance, and a whole lot of cozy! Book two is slated for a 2021 release!

Ms. McDonald resides on her Thoroughbred farm known as Fly by Night Stables near Pittsburgh, Pennsylvania, with her husband, Bill, and her poorly behaved Cocker Spaniel, Allister.

You can learn more about C.S. McDonald and her books here: **www.csmcdonaldbooks.com**

More cozy mysteries by C.S. McDonald:

The Fiona Quinn Mysteries
Murder on Pointe
Merry Murder
Waves of Murder
Tastes Like Murder
Good Luck to Murder
Mambo and Murder
Saddle Up for Murder
Bon Voyage to Murder
Taking Notes on Murder

Short stories by C.S. McDonald:

Fiona Quinn QUICK Mysteries
"Banking on a Murder"
"Harriet's Heist"

"Crystal Clear Confusion"
"The Christmas Cameo"

Thank you to these wonderful services:

Cover design: DusktilDawn Designs
Editor: Sherri Good, Silver Lining Editing Services
Proofreader: Renee Waring, Guardian Proofreading

Made in the USA
Monee, IL
04 October 2025

30533734R00115